MISTER BIG

Behind all the large-scale crimes of recent years, the police believe there is an organising genius. The name by which this mysterious personality has become familiar to the press, the police and the underworld is Mister Big. When murder and kidnapping are added to his crimes, Superintendent Budd of Scotland Yard becomes actively involved. Eventually the master detective uncovers a witness who has actually observed and recognised Mister Big leaving the scene of a murder — but before he can tell Budd whom he has seen, he is himself murdered!

GERALD VERNER

◆

MISTER BIG

Complete and Unabridged

LINFORD
Leicester

First published in Great Britain

First Linford Edition
published 2015

The characters in this story are entirely fictitious
and bear no relation to any living person.

A catalogue record for this book is available
from the British Library.

ISBN 978–1–4448–2485–8

Published by
F. A. Thorpe (Publishing)
Anstey, Leicestershire

Set by Words & Graphics Ltd.
Anstey, Leicestershire
Printed and bound in Great Britain by
T. J. International Ltd., Padstow, Cornwall

This book is printed on acid-free paper

1

Gordon Trent pulled a typed sheet from the typewriter, inserted another blank sheet from the pile at his elbow, and began to beat a staccato tattoo on the keys. Through the partly open window the sound of Big Ben floated into the room. Gordon grunted as he discovered that it was already half past ten. The messenger would be calling for his 'copy' from the *Post-Bulletin* at eleven and there was still quite a lot to finish.

His fingers flew faster over the keys and another page was added to the scattered collection on the desk in front of him.

The room in which he was working was rather shabby and untidy, but conveyed an air of comfort that was very pleasing.

Trent was still on the right side of thirty, but during his short life he had done many things. He had been an actor, been secretary to a wealthy stockbroker, a job which had terminated suddenly when his employer had been sentenced to five years for fraud, had run a typewriting bureau that flourished spasmodically until a mounting collection of bad debts had closed it down, and finally drifted to Fleet Street.

And after a long struggle he had made the grade. At the age of twenty-eight he had an assured income and the comforting knowledge that ninety per cent of what he wrote would be accepted.

Stopping for a moment from his labours he reached for a cigarette, stuck it between his lips, lit it, and was pounding again at the typewriter when the front door bell rang. It rang twice, but Gordon oblivious of external sounds went on with his work. There was a pause and then the bell again more insistently.

'Blast!' muttered Gordon irritably. 'It must be that infernal messenger!'

He pushed back his chair and struggled to his feet, running his fingers through his unruly hair. Without putting on his jacket he crossed the room and went out into the small hall. Jerking open the front door he was preparing to tell the disturber of his peace a few home truths. But the words died on his lips and he only managed to utter a strangled gurgle as he saw his visitor.

It was a girl and she smiled as he gaped foolishly at her.

'I'm terribly sorry to disturb you, Mr. Trent,' she apologised, 'but I knew you were in because I could see the light under your door when I looked through the letter-box.'

'It's quite all right' stammered Gordon aghast at what he had been about to call the bell ringer, 'I'm very glad to be disturbed — that is — what can I do for you.' He became acutely aware of his shirtsleeves and the unruliness of his hair. 'I — I didn't expect anyone — that is . . . ' He quavered to an uneasy silence.

The girl outside the door smiled — a sympathetic and understanding smile.

'I wouldn't have bothered you,' she said, 'only Father's gone over to the House and he's forgotten to take his latchkey. I've just had a telephone message from a friend who has been taken ill and wants me to go and see her

3

at once. It's rather a long way and Father is sure to get home first. I was wondering if you would give him the key when he comes in?'

She held out a Yale key.

'Of course, I will,' said Gordon.

She dropped the little key into his open palm.

'It's awfully good of you,' she said gratefully. 'I was sure you would so I phoned and told Father to call for it.'

'You're sure there's nothing else I can do?' asked Gordon.

She shook her head.

'Except tell Father I'll be back as soon as I can and not to sit up for me.'

She drew her coat round her and turned away.

'Good-night, Mr. Trent,' she said. 'And thank you again.'

'Only too pleased, Miss Stayner,' he declared heartily. 'Good-night.'

He watched her as she ran lightly down the stairs, her fair hair gleaming in the light of the overhead staircase lighting. She looked back and waved as she rounded the first bend and then was

4

gone. Gordon shut the front door and went back to his sitting-room. But he found that his concentration had suffered from his visitant. His thoughts kept wandering to the girl who had just left.

The daughter of John Stayner, M.P., who occupied the flat above Trent's had gradually become a very considerable factor in his life and for many weeks had disturbed his thoughts as she was disturbing them now. Several chance meetings on the stairs or in the lift, which was always going wrong, had been the basis of an acquaintance that Gordon was determined should ripen into something more. The acquaintanceship had extended to Stayner who had got into the habit of dropping in for a drink and a chat now and again. Once Gordon had taken Margaret to the theatre and for one entire evening had lived in a world that contained only one slim girl whose eyes were the bluest he had ever seen. In fact, Gordon Trent was undergoing all the symptoms of falling in love.

But there was only ten minutes before the messenger was due to pick up the 'copy' and he had to thrust all other thoughts from his mind and finish it. The last page coincided with the arrival of the messenger, and with a sigh of relief Gordon clipped the typed sheets together, thrust them into an envelope and gave them to the man.

'That's that,' muttered Gordon when the man had gone. He lighted a cigarette and poured himself out a stiff Johnnie Walker. Putting the key of the Stayners' flat on the mantelpiece he carried his drink over to the armchair and sat down. He had intended to complete a short story but the girl's visit had acted as a disturbing influence. He wondered who the 'friend', was who had been taken ill. Gordon tried to recollect the names of some of the girl's friends but he couldn't think of any. Whoever it was must have been on very intimate terms to send for Margaret like that . . .

Quite suddenly he realised that behind this interest in what was, after all, a trivial occurrence, there lurked a certain uneasiness. Yes, that was the exact word — uneasiness. For no reason that he could account for he felt a sense of alarm.

The whole thing was ridiculous, he thought irritably. Why should he be alarmed? It was a very natural thing for a friend who was ill to ask another friend to go and see them. It was absurd that he should feel this uneasiness. But he couldn't shake it off.

He got up and poured himself out another whisky. As he poured in a little water the front-door bell rang. It rang in a curious jerky manner, as though the hand of the person pressing the button was trembling violently. Gordon put down his drink.

That must be old Stayner come to fetch his key, he thought, crossing the room. It sounds as if he'd had one over the eight . . .

He reached the front door and opened it. At first he could see nothing for the landing light had been extinguished and then he made out the dim shape of a man who was half-crouching on the threshold. Gordon stared at him in astonishment. The man staggered to his feet and swayed through the open door into the hall. He looked like a tramp. His clothes were ragged and stained, his shoes broken and gaping.

He tottered past Gordon, staring back over his shoulder with eyes that were wide with fear.

'Here, what the deuce are you doing?' demanded Gordon. 'You've made a mistake . . . '

The intruder shook his head weakly; groped his way to the sitting-room door, pushed it open and entered. Gordon, with pardonable annoyance followed him. The stranger sank down in an easy chair in utter exhaustion, but as Gordon came in he started up and pointed a shaking hand to the door.

'Shut it!' he croaked hoarsely. 'For the love of God shut the door!'

'Look here!' began Gordon, but the other interrupted him.

'Shut the door!' he repeated insistently, his breath coming in great choking gasps. 'There's death — outside.'

The effort was too much for him and he collapsed back into the chair with his head lolling forward on his chest.

Convinced that he was dealing with a lunatic but thinking it would be better to humour the man, Gordon went out and slammed the front door. When he came back the other was breathing heavily and with difficulty but he managed to raise his head as Gordon approached the chair.

'Is it shut?' he whispered eagerly. 'Nobody — can — get in?'

'Not unless they wriggle through the keyhole,' answered Gordon sarcastically. 'Now, what's all this about? Who are you?'

'Don't you know me?' whispered the stranger.

'No, of course I don't . . . ' began Gordon.

'Jameson . . . Charterhouse.'

The words were barely audible. The rasping of the breathing more pronounced. Gordon started. Bending down he peered into the emaciated face upturned to his own.

'Good God, so it is!' he exclaimed incredulously.

The other's dry lips curved into the beginning of a thin smile, and then a spasm of agony contorted the mouth and his hands went up to his throat.

'Brandy!' came a strangled gasp. 'Brandy!'

Gordon went to the sideboard, took out a bottle of Hennessy from the cupboard, and poured out a generous portion into a glass. Hurrying back to the chair he uttered an exclamation. Jameson no longer sat up but had slumped sideways over the arm. His eyes were closed and his lips parted. His breathing was now almost imperceptible.

'Jameson!' cried Gordon sharply. 'Here, drink this!'

He held the glass to the cracked lips and tried to pull the man up to a sitting posture, but the body was limp and unresponsive.

'What the devil had I better do?' muttered Gordon, trying to rouse some semblance of life but without result. And then an idea struck him.

'Dr. Smedhurst, of course!' he exclaimed.

Putting down the glass of brandy, he rushed out into the hall, jerked open the front door, and went stumbling down the dark stairway to the floor below . . .

In the room he had just left there was silence except for the faint hiss of breath from the man in the chair and the ticking of the clock on the mantelpiece. Then the man called Jameson shuddered violently, opened his eyes and stared wildly round. Shaking violently, he sat up, passing a thin hand over his eyes. After a moment he rose dizzily to his feet, clutching the back of the chair for support. For a second or two he stood swaying, his breath rasping through his clenched teeth, and then with uncertain steps he began to grope his way over to the writing-table.

Reaching it, he paused to recover a little from his exertions and then picked up the pencil that lay on the blotting-pad. Gripping the edge of the table with his left hand for support, he began to scribble feverishly on the topmost sheet of the pile of blank paper. He had succeeded in scrawling one wavering line when the sound of a violent knocking somewhere below made him start so violently that he almost dropped the pencil. He looked round with fear-filled eyes towards the door and then with a supreme effort forced himself to go on with his task.

There was a slight sound from the hall and the light went out. A hand groped round the edge of the door, a gloved hand feeling for the light switch.

The man at the writing-table uttered a squeal of terror as the light in the room went out, too, and swung round to face the door, clutching the paper he had been writing on to his breast.

'Oh, my God!' he breathed, and began to sob jerkily.

A smudge of shadow spread from the door towards him. Two questing hands found his throat, fastened there and squeezed. It was all over in a few seconds. And now there was only the sound of the clock ticking to break the silence of the room . . .

2

'Shakespeare,' remarked Mr. Budd wearily, 'is a very over-rated feller.'

Sergeant Leek, perched on a hard chair in the stout superintendent's office in Scotland Yard, raised a pair of tired eyes and looked across at his superior.

'What's his line?' he asked with an effort to appear interested.

'What d'you mean?' demanded Mr. Budd.

'What is this feller? What's 'e do?'

Mr. Budd regarded him with an expression of disapproval on his fat face.

'I don't know,' he said, shaking his head. 'I really *don't* know! How you ever got into the C.I.D. at all beats me. Your ignorance is appalling!'

Sergeant Leek wilted under a withering gaze. It was not entirely due to Mr. Budd's reprimand, for he had been in a gradual process of wilting since eleven o'clock and it was now past midnight.

'What is 'e, then?' he asked in an injured voice 'A burglar, con man, or one of this 'ere bank robbers?'

'He isn't anything,' answered Mr. Budd shifting his huge bulk into a more comfortable position. 'He's dead!'

'Somebody do 'im, eh?' said the sergeant brightly, feeling that this might be safe ground.

Mr. Budd snorted irritably.

'Shakespeare was a poet,' he growled.

'Oh!' Leek's intonation conveyed the impression that this was worse than anything he had imagined. 'I thought you was talkin' about a crook.'

'There's only one real crook in existence,' snapped Mr. Budd, and the sergeant had no need this time to ask to whom he referred. 'Mister Big' had during the past months become a major problem with the police throughout the country.

'My reference to Shakespeare,' continued Mr. Budd, ' 'ad nothin' to do with crim'nals. It was concerned with roses.'

The lean sergeant was not interested. He knew little about poets or roses, having for many years lived in a back street off the Kennington Road which is not an ideal locality for studying either. However, if his superior wished to talk about these subjects it was as well to listen with a certain degree of enforced interest. He tried, therefore, to infuse some kind of enthusiasm into his tired voice when he replied:

'What's roses got ter do with it?'

'Shakespeare stated that 'a rose by any other name would smell as sweet.' A ridic'lous statement!' affirmed the super-intendent.

'I don't see why,' said Leek.

'That's because you've got no soul,' declared Mr. Budd with a gesture that effectually disposed of any small amount of soul the sergeant might have. 'Take a look at those.' He turned his eyes toward a vase of tea roses that stood on his desk and which had come from his own garden. 'Would they be the same if they was called onions?'

'Wouldn't make no difference to the smell if you called 'em pick-axes,' argued Leek truthfully.

Mr. Budd regarded him with a hard and stony eye.

'There is no smell to a pick-axe,' he retorted.

Leek was trying to think of something further to say on this absorbing subject when the clock on the wall struck the hour.

'It doesn't look as if this feller's comin',' he growled.

'Gabby's generally to be relied on,' said Leek glad to change the subject.

Mr. Budd dipped his forefinger and thumb into his pocket and produced one of his thin black cigars.

'No 'grass' can ever be relied on,' he grunted, sniffing at the cigar. 'That's my experience. I don't see why Gabby Smith should be any different to the rest of 'em. You say he's got special information about this Big man?'

'Yes.' The sergeant nodded. 'He said he'd know who he was this evenin'. Somethin' must've 'appened to delay him.'

'You get brighter an' brighter every day!' said Mr. Budd sarcastically. He reached out for a match and carefully lit his cigar, blowing out clouds of evil-smelling smoke. 'If you go on at this rate they'll be makin' you an inspector before you know where you are!'

The long thin face of the sergeant assumed an expression of hurt resignation. His lack of promotion was a sore point with him. In his own mind he was convinced that he should have attained the highest possible rank by this time and the reason he hadn't was sheer jealousy on the part of his superiors who were afraid that he might outshine them all if he were given the chance. He ignored Mr. Budd's biting remarks, knowing from experience that the stout superintendent did not mean any unkindness.

'It'll be worth waitin' for if Gabby can tell us who this Big man is, won't it?' said Leek after a pause.

Mr. Budd nodded ponderously, closed his eyes and sent a stream of smoke towards the ceiling.

There came a tap at the door and a uniformed constable entered. He laid a dirty crumpled envelope on the desk in front of Mr. Budd.

'This was left for you, sir,' he said. 'The man who brought it said there was no answer.'

Mr. Budd picked up the stained envelope and slit it open with a fat forefinger. It contained a single sheet of cheap paper. Glancing rapidly at the hasty, ill-spelt message, the superintendent shrugged his massive shoulders.

'So much for Gabby Smith,' he grunted, flipping the message over to Leek, and relapsed into his previous lethargic state. 'You can go, Collins.'

The constable withdrew and Leek read the brief note, his long face growing longer as he puzzled it out.

Have not got infermashun. To dangerus to come. Being watched. G.S.

Without comment the sergeant put it down.

'We may as well go home,' remarked Mr. Budd. 'I thought it sounded too easy; just sit here an' wait for Smith to come an' tell us the identity of Mister Big.' He shook his head. 'Too easy. We shan't catch the feller that way.'

He gripped the edge of his desk and hoisted himself laboriously out of his chair.

'You look as if some sleep 'ud do you good,' he remarked as he took down his coat from the peg and struggled into it.

'I could sleep standin' up!' declared Leek fervently, uncoiling his long length from the chair and stretching.

'You usually do!' retorted the stout superintendent.

Before the sergeant could think of a reply to this, the telephone bell rang.

'Now what is it, I wonder?' growled Mr. Budd. He put the receiver to his ear. The call was from the officer in charge of the night staff and the weary Leek saw Mr. Budd's face change.

'All right, I'll get round there in three minutes,' he snapped. 'No, I'll take Sergeant Leek with me. Tell 'em not to touch anythin' until we get there.'

He slammed down the receiver.

'You won't get any sleep yet,' he said to his yawning subordinate. 'There's been a murder at Wellington Mansions in Victoria Street. A man's been killed in a flat belongin' to a feller called Gordon Trent. From what I can make out Mister Big's got somethin' to do with it.'

Mr. Budd plucked a rose from the vase, inserted it in the lapel of his overcoat, and went over to the door.

'How do you know the Big man's got anythin' to do with it?' asked Leek as he followed.

'Pure deduction!' growled Mr. Budd as they hurried along the corridor to the lift. 'A torn scrap of paper with the words 'Mister Big' scrawled on it was found in the dead man's hand!'

3

The advent of the person known as 'Mister Big' as a public menace had been gradual, mixing with the ordinary routine of life much as drop of pungent pigment will slowly colour a quantity of water. Various stories and rumours began to reach the ears of the police. Little crooks, pulled in for various small offences, spoke of the Big Man, the Planner, the Boss Man, but remained silent when they were asked for further information.

Others, higher up the social scale of organised villainy, smiled when they too were questioned but maintained a dumbness equal to their lesser confreres. The police rightly, look askance at the possibility of a master criminal, experience telling them that outside the covers of sensational novels there is no such thing. But it became increasingly obvious that there did exist someone who planned a number of the major robberies. This person who became known as Mister Big, ruled by fear and had only one way of dealing with those who sought to betray him — the way Al Dane, the jewel thief had gone, when in a moment of drunken expansiveness and tempted by the reward he had been promised to lead a squad of detectives to the place where Mister Big could be found. Dane had been in the act of stepping into the police car outside Scotland Yard when a bullet put an end to his career.

Who had fired the shot or whence it came was never discovered, for the shooter had used a silencer, and there had been a stream of pedestrians and motor traffic passing at the time.

The incident had proved that Mister Big was not just someone who had been imagined by a handful of crooks but a real and potent force behind the crime wave that had to be reckoned with.

Inquiries were set afoot by patient men who worked night and day to lift the veil which shrouded the man's identity but results were meagre. At the end of sixteen months, during which period a number of daring, and well-planned raids involving many thousands of pounds were carried out, they had made little progress. Mister Big remained a name and nothing more.

Squads of detectives haunted night-spots and public houses, clip-joints and such places where criminals of all classes frequent, questioning, cajolling, threatening. But at the mention of Mister Big there would come instant silence and a half fearful glance over the shoulder. The fate of Al Dane was remembered and acted as an awful example.

The main reason for Mister Big's continued obscurity can be attributed to the fact that he did not control a gang. He took his choice from those who were most suitable for the job in hand. When he had finished with them they were paid off and dispersed.

In this way there was no one group of people associated with him. Mr. Budd had been put in charge of the campaign to find this formidable menace and had been unable to make any headway. Every fresh line he tackled ended in a blind alley.

The crime wave in London and the surrounding districts took an upward trend and behind each fresh outrage could be seen the directing hand that had planned it. But no one could give a name to the owner of that hand — except the fanciful one of 'Mister Big.' Behind the screen of that name lurked a powerful personality, clever enough to keep his identity secret even from those he employed.

Mr. Budd had hoped, though with less optimism than Sergeant Leek, that Gabby Smith might provide the information he sought, but the informer had failed him. Perhaps this murder at Wellington Mansions would yield something.

He turned into the entrance to the flats, followed by the weary Leek, who looked even more lugubrious than usual. The lift wasn't working and they had to climb the stone stair. There was an open door on the third landing from which a wedge-shaped light fanned out.

'That'll be the place,' panted Mr. Budd, breathless from the exertion of the staircase. 'An' if you ask me how I know, it's just deduction!'

He stabbed at the bell-push with a fat finger, and Gordon appeared in the hall. His hair was rumpled and his face white and strained.

'I'm glad you've come!' he exclaimed when Mr. Budd had introduced himself. 'Come in! I scarcely know whether I'm awake or dreaming.'

'Sergeant Leek will sympathise with you,' grunted Mr. Budd. 'That's his natural state!'

They followed Gordon across the small hall to the room from which he had emerged.

Two men were standing silently by the fireplace and looked up as they came in.

Trent introduced them.

'This is Mr. John Stayner who lives in the flat above,' he said, indicating the taller of the two, a military-looking man with grey hair, 'and this is Dr. Smedhurst.'

The other man nodded curtly. He was large-boned and loosely built; his clothes fitted him badly. His face was rugged and his jaw was underslung. Mr. Budd summed him up as a man who it would be unpleasant to have as an enemy.

'This is a nasty business, superintendent,' said the grey-haired man in a deep, pleasant voice. His eyes flickered to the huddled form near the writing-table and flickered away again.

'All murder is unpleasant,' said Mr. Budd, allowing his eyes to travel slowly round the room. 'Though you'd think these days that the murderer was somethin' to be coddled an' respected. That's what we call progress! We don't care a hoot about the victim. It's the killer who gets all the sympathy.' He went over and looked down at the dead man. 'Is this how 'e was found?'

'Practically.' It was the doctor who answered. 'I may have moved him slightly when I made my examination.'

Mr. Budd bent down and peered at the upturned throat and the congested face.

'Looks as if he was strangled,' he murmured. He pointed to the bluish bruises on the skin.

'He was,' said Smedhurst. 'Those are the marks of the murderer's fingers. No very great pressure was necessary in his weak state.'

'No?' Mr. Budd caressed his fat chin

with an equally fat hand. 'Starved was he?'

'Partly,' agreed the doctor. 'Mostly due to drugs, I think.'

'Drugs, eh?' The stout superintendent raised his eyes sleepily and looked up. 'A drug addict, was he?'

'I'm pretty sure of it,' answered Smedhurst.

'You must be wrong,' interposed Gordon quickly. 'Ronald Jameson was the last chap to take drugs . . . '

'I'm only going by the condition of the body.' Smedhurst shrugged his shoulders. 'His whole system is saturated with heroin . . . '

'Then it was given to him,' said Trent. 'I'm certain he would never have taken it himself.'

Mr. Budd, still gently scratching his chin, turned wearily towards the emphatic young man.

'Look here,' he remarked almost apologetically, 'suppose you tell me exactly what happened.'

Gordon ran his fingers through his already untidy hair, hesitated for a second, and then plunged into an account of what had happened up to the time he had gone to fetch Dr. Smedhurst.

'I was some time making the doctor hear,' he concluded. 'When I got back with him the whole place was in darkness. Jameson was lying just as he is now.'

'You left the light on in the hall?'

'Yes, both in the hall and in here.'

Mr. Budd went over to the lamp on the writing-table and regarded it with a frown as though it had offended him, he looked up at the centre pendant, and then at the switch by the door.

'Are both lights controlled from the switch?' he asked.

'Yes. There's a separate switch on the table lamp,' said Gordon. 'That switch puts 'em both out.'

'You can't put on the table lamp without putting on the centre one as well?'

'No. I've been going to have it altered but I've never got around to it.'

'Must be quite awkward,' murmured the big man. He sighed. His expression was one of infinite boredom. 'I see. An' they was both out when you came back with the doctor?'

Trent nodded.

'How long were you away?'

'About three minutes, possibly four.'

'Durin' that time someone came in through the front door which you had left open, turned out all the lights, an' killed this feller — what's his name?'

'Jameson.'

'Quick work,' remarked Mr. Budd pursing his thick lips. 'Remarkably quick work. Your friend must've been followed here.

'I think he was and he knew it,' said Gordon. He repeated what the dead man had said.

'There *was* death outside — for him,' murmured Mr. Budd. He sniffed gently at the rose in his button-hole. 'Why did he come here to-night?'

'I don't know. I haven't the least idea. I've not seen or heard of him for over five years. He was so changed I didn't recognise him at first . . . '

'Five years is a long time. I don't suppose I'd recognise Leek in five years.' He looked across at the melancholy sergeant who was leaning against the doorpost waiting sleepily for orders. And he got them.

'There's a cab-rank within sight of the entrance to these flats,' said Mr. Budd. 'Go down an' have a word with the drivers. Ask 'em if they noticed who went in an' out of these flats durin' the past hour.'

Sergeant Leek yawned and detached himself from the doorpost.

'Find out, if you can, if a car or a taxi stopped here round about eleven,' went on Mr. Budd. 'I'd ask you to hurry only I know it's against your principles!'

Leek gave him a reproachful look but without a word went out. Mr. Budd turned to Gordon.

'There was a paper or somethin' found in the dead man's hand, wasn't there?' he asked. 'I'd like to see it.'

'Here you are.' Trent went over to the writing-table and picked up a small jagged piece of paper from the blotting-pad. Mr. Budd took it from him and regarded it with a fishy eye.

'H'm,' he remarked. 'Not much here.' He laboriously deciphered the wavering writing. ' 'Tell the . . . ' Then there's a bit missin' an' then the words 'Mister Big.' After that it looks as if his pencil had slipped.' He sighed. 'That's when he was interrupted an' strangled.' He shook his head regretfully. 'I'd give a lot to know the rest of the message.'

'The murderer tore it out of the dead man's hand,' put in Dr. Smedhurst. 'Thought he'd got it all, I suppose.'

'Did you take this piece from his hand?' The doctor nodded.

'I wish you hadn't,' continued Mr. Budd. 'I wish you'd left it where it was. I don't suppose he was fool enough to leave any prints but if he did you've obliterated 'em.' He sighed again. 'I'll get our fellers to look at it, anyhow.' He put the scrap carefully away in his wallet. 'Maybe there's somethin' in his pockets that'll help us.'

He knelt down with difficulty and made a quick but thorough search.

'Nothin' at all,' he grunted disappointedly and scratched his head. 'Now that's very curious.'

'Why?' asked Stayner. He removed his arm from the mantelpiece on which he had been leaning and came over.

'It's curious because most people carry *somethin'* in their pockets, don't they, sir?'

Mr. Budd rising from his knees dusted the knees of his trousers with great care. 'You wouldn't find even a tramp without somethin'.'

'The man who killed him took whatever there was, I expect,' said the M.P.

'I doubt it,' disagreed Mr. Budd. 'He wouldn't have had the time. You say you hadn't seen Jameson for five years?'

'About that,' answered Trent.

'Where did you last see him?'

'At the Berkley Grill. We dined together before he left for Germany on the following day.'

'Germany?' Mr. Budd looked surprised. 'What was he going to Germany for?'

'Jameson was a chemist,' explained Gordon. 'He was going to Germany to study some new experiments that were being carried out in West Berlin. I don't know what they were — he didn't tell me.'

'Did you hear from him while he was away?'

'One very short note to say that he'd arrived and was very busy.'

The superintendent examined his fat thumb with great interest.

'You didn't hear or see anythin' of him again until he turned up here to-night?' he asked after a pause.

'Nothing!' declared Gordon. 'You wouldn't be surprised if you'd known Jameson. He hated writing letters.'

'I knew a feller like that,' said Mr. Budd. 'This feller never wrote to anyone unless he wanted somethin' an' then he'd forget to post it! Any family?'

'Jameson? No, he was an orphan. There was an uncle somewhere, I believe, but he died while we were at Charterhouse.'

'Wasn't married, I suppose?'

Gordon shook his head.

'Not as far as I know.'

Mr. Budd nodded several times and his eyelids began to droop. He looked as if he was in imminent danger of falling asleep, but after a moment his eyes opened again.

'How was he off for money?' he asked.

'I never knew anything about his

private affairs,' answered Trent. 'He always seemed to have plenty of money.'

'It doesn't look as though he'd had much lately,' murmured Mr. Budd glancing at the shabby figure by the writing-table. Then, almost to himself, he added : 'I wonder what he knew about Mister Big.'

'Who is this 'Mister Big'?' asked Stayner.

'I wish I could tell you, sir,' said Mr. Budd fervently. 'Nothin' would give me greater pleasure, I assure you.' He walked over to the writing-table. 'I'd like to use your phone,' he said, and without waiting for permission picked up the receiver.

His conversation was short.

'The photographers an' fingerprint men 'ull be here very soon,' he said unnecessarily for they had heard him. 'I wonder what's happened to my sergeant. Maybe he's fallen asleep somewhere. He thinks all the time he's awake is time wasted.'

But the lean sergeant was very much awake. He came in almost as Mr. Budd finished speaking, accompanied by a thick-set man with a remarkably red face, and swathed in a voluminous overcoat that added several inches to his girth.

'This man's been on the rank most of the evenin',' announced Leek, 'an' bein' naturally of a curious disposition he can tell you everybody who went or came out of these flats up to a few minutes ago.'

The red-faced taxi-driver nodded his agreement with this statement.

'That's right,' he said in a husky whisper. 'From eight o'clock I bin stuck on that blasted rank. People don't want cabs like what they used to. There weren't nobody up to a few minutes past eleven. Then a young woman in a fur coat came out o' these 'ere flats an' drove away in Sam 'Iggins' cab . . . '

'That was my daughter,' put in John Stayner. 'She was on her way to visit a friend who was taken ill.'

Gordon suddenly realised that in the general excitement he had forgotten about the girl. Now that he had been reminded he experienced once more that vague uneasiness. He kept silent, however, and the taxi-driver went on:

'Well, after she'd gone,' he said, speaking with the deliberation of his kind, 'another chap called, and then old Jack, the porter, left to go 'ome. 'E stopped an' 'ad a word with me, like 'e usually do, if I'm on the rank. I didn't see another blinkin' soul until just after twenty past eleven when a chap come staggerin' down Victoria Street, 'alf runnin' an' 'alf walkin'. 'E was a shabby feller, looked drunk to me. I was surprised when 'e turned in 'ere . . . '

He broke off as for the first time he became aware of the man by the writing-table.

'Cor lummy!' he ejaculated, staring. 'Why that's 'im! That's the chap! 'Ere what's 'appened?'

'Did you see anyone else?' broke in Mr. Budd impatiently.

The taxi-driver dragged his fascinated gaze away from the body.

'Yes, I did,' he asserted. 'I seed a bloke come down the street arter 'im an' follow 'im in 'ere . . . '

'Can you describe this man?' asked Mr. Budd.

'I can do more than that,' wheezed the taxi-driver triumphantly. 'I can tell yer who 'e was!'

'You know him?' Mr. Budd's voice was unusually excited.

'I should say so,' said the taxi-driver. But that was as far as he got. There was a commotion in the hall and then the door swung open and a girl stumbled dazedly into the room.

'Good God — Margaret!' cried Gordon. 'What's the matter? What's happened . . . ?'

There was good reason for his question. The girl's coat was torn and covered in mud. Her sheer nylon stockings were in shreds and her hair was wet and hung in strands over her dirty face. There was a large purple bruise on her forehead and across one cheek was a cut that was oozing blood. Swaying dizzily she grasped the doorframe for support, tried vainly to speak, and then before either Trent or John Stayner could reach her, slid down on the floor and lay still.

4

Doctor Smedhurst was the first to reach the unconscious girl. After a quick examination he looked up at the others.

'She's fainted — that's all,' he announced reassuringly. 'Nothing serious. She seems to have been in some sort of accident. Help me get her on to that settee.'

It was Gordon and Stayner who picked up the limp body of the girl and put it down gently on the settee. The M.P. looked worried and anxious.

'How did she get like this?' he asked, but since nobody knew they couldn't answer him. Gordon, anxious and fearful, hovered round the girl, not knowing quite what to do.

Mr. Budd looked round at the gaping taxi-driver who was standing near, an interested and astonished spectator.

'You wait in the hall,' he ordered. 'I shall want you again in a moment.'

The man nodded. He took off his cap,

scratched his head vigorously, and went out into the little hall.

'Get some water,' said Stayner, as he put a cushion under the girl's head.

'I'll get some,' said Smedhurst.

'The kitchen's at the end of the hall,' put in Trent, and the doctor hurried out. In a few minutes he returned with a glass of water. Gordon took it from him and tried to force a few drops between the girl's lips. Dipping his handkerchief in the remainder he gently bathed her forehead.

'She's coming round,' said Stayner as the girl's eyelids quivered and she uttered a sigh.

'An' I'll bet the first thing she says is 'where am I?'' murmured Mr. Budd to himself, but he was wrong.

Margaret opened her eyes slowly and stared up vacantly at Stayner and Gordon who were bending anxiously over her but without any sign of recognition. Then she smiled faintly and her lips parted as though she were trying to say something. No sound escaped her but the second attempt was more successful. She began to speak almost inaudibly.

'I — I couldn't get any further,' she whispered with an obvious effort. 'I — couldn't . . . ' Her voice trailed away incoherently.

'I'll get some brandy,' said Gordon.

He went over to the sideboard and picked up the bottle of Hennessy and poured out a generous portion.

'Drink some of this, Margaret,' he said coming back to the settee. He held the glass for her and she drank some of the brandy. The effect was soon apparent. A tinge of colour crept into her cheeks and when she spoke her voice was stronger.

'I tried — to reach — our flat above,' she said, 'but I couldn't make it. I suddenly — felt so dizzy . . . ' She stopped and put up a hand to her head. 'My — head . . . It aches terribly,' she complained.

'What happened, my dear?' asked Stayner. 'How did you get in this state?'

'There was an accident,' she said, her voice gaining strength. 'My taxi ran into a car . . . nobody was hurt badly . . . I was thrown out of the door.'

'Then you haven't been to Eileen's?' said Stayner.

She started to shake her head and winced.

'I never got as far. I was on my way when the accident happened. The car came out of a side turning . . . I wish you'd phone to Eileen, daddy, and let her know . . . '

'Are you sure you're not hurt?' broke in Gordon.

'Not really. I'm a bit bruised.'

'How did you get back?'

'In a taxi.' She smiled. 'I was terrified we might have another accident.'

Mr. Budd, who had hitherto been silent, now spoke.

'If I was you, miss,' he remarked, 'I'd get to bed as soon as possible.'

He was standing behind the girl and he gave Stayner a significant glance. The M.P. grasped his meaning at once. Margaret had seen nothing of the dead man in the shadow of the writing-table. At any moment the photographers, the fingerprint men, and the police doctor would arrive and all the routine of an investigation into wilful murder get under way. Mr. Budd was anxious that the girl

41

should see nothing of all this.

'That's a very good suggestion of yours,' said Stayner. 'I'll go and switch on the electric fires if you'll bring Margaret up, Trent?'

Gordon nodded.

'I'll look after her,' he said.

'What about phoning Eileen?' asked the girl as he put out his hand to open the door.

'We can do that upstairs,' said the M.P. and went out closing the door behind him.

Gordon helped the girl to raise herself to a sitting position. He made her swallow a little more brandy and then assisted her to her feet. She was still a little weak but she clung to his arm and managed to walk slowly to the door.

'Take it easy,' said Gordon. 'There's no hurry.'

'All I want is a hot bath and bed,' she answered. 'I shall be all right tomorrow.'

He guided her to the door and Dr. Smedhurst opened it. As they went out, Mr. Budd relaxed.

'Now,' he said, 'we'll have another word

with that taxi-driver.'

He called him but there was no reply. Going out into the lobby he saw that the man had fallen asleep.

'Here, wake up!' said Mr. Budd, and shook him gently by the shoulder. The man rolled sideways and fell heavily to the floor.

The stout superintendent uttered a sharp exclamation. Bending over the fallen man, he drew in his breath with a little hiss as he saw the handle of the knife which had been driven to the hilt between the man's shoulder-blades and which glinted redly in the dim light of the overhead bulb.

The taxi-driver was dead!

5

'What's the matter?'

Attracted by the superintendent's sudden ejaculation, Doctor Smedhurst came out of the sitting-room. He caught sight of the man sprawled on the floor and said sharply:

'What's happened? Is he ill?'

'He's dead!' snapped Mr. Budd harshly, and then as Leek followed the doctor: 'Mister Big has been a busy man to-night.'

'What do you mean?' Smedhurst's large face changed. The muscles of his heavy jaw contracted. 'You mean that . . . ?'

'I mean this man was murdered!' retorted Mr. Budd. He pointed to the knife that projected from the dead man's back. 'Don't touch it!' he added quickly as the doctor moved over. 'There may be prints.'

'This is dreadful,' said Smedhurst, peering down. 'When did it happen — while we were all here?'

Mr. Budd nodded.

'Must've. The front door wasn't shut. He must've come in while we were occupied with that girl.'

'He was all right when I went to fetch the water,' asserted Smedhurst. 'He looked up as I passed.'

He bent down and touched the cold wrist and lifted one of the eyelids.

'He's dead right enough . . . '

'Yes, he's dead right enough,' repeated Mr. Budd. 'I didn't think he was anythin' else. Mister Big doesn't do things by halves.'

The doctor looked at him curiously.

'Why should this man — what do you call him? — Mister Big — why should he want to kill this poor fellow?'

'Self-preservation,' answered Mr. Budd. 'The biggest motive in the world, eh? This man saw too much.'

'Of course!' ejaculated the doctor. 'He was going to tell you who the man was who followed Jameson in here.'

'He was,' agreed Mr. Budd sadly, 'an' if that girl hadn't turned up when she did, he would've done. If she'd have come just a minute later we'd have had the name.' He sighed. 'Oh, well, it can't be helped now.'

'How did the murderer know that this man had seen and recognised him?' demanded Doctor Smedhurst frowning. 'Or that he was going to give him away?'

'Maybe, he saw my sergeant talkin' to the man, guessed that he'd seen somethin', and when they came up here, he followed and listened. That blasted front door again. It ought to have been shut.'

'Surely Miss Stayner would have seen him?' suggested the doctor, but the superintendent shook his head. When he spoke the excitement had died from his voice and it had reverted to its habitual lazy drawl.

'She wasn't well enough to notice anythin',' he said, 'an' it was dark on the landin'. I wish those fellers I sent for 'ud hurry up. If there's one thing I hate it's bein' kept . . . '

He broke off as there came the sound of feet on the staircase outside. The bell rang and then the front door was pushed open and a man peered in.

46

'Is this . . . ?' he began, but Mr. Budd interrupted before he could say any more.

'Come in, Smithers,' he said. 'Nice to see you! What have you been up to, eh? Havin' a joy ride round London?'

A thin little man came into the dim light of the hall.

'Waiting for the D.S.,' answered Smithers with a grin. 'Dr. Salisbury was attending a drunk . . . '

'And remarkably drunk he was,' said a cheerful voice belonging to a jovial, stoutish man who came in followed by a third man with a large bag. 'What's been happening here?'

Mr. Budd told him briefly and the divisional-surgeon whistled.

'Mister Big, eh?' He made a grimace. 'It's about time you people put a spoke in his wheel. I'll have a look at the other one first. Then these chaps can get on with their photographs and dabs. In here?' He nodded towards the dor of the sitting-room.

'That's right,' said Mr. Budd.

'You won't want me, will you?' asked Doctor Smedhurst as the three men trooped into the sitting-room. 'I'd like to go back to my flat downstairs.'

'Oh, yes, of course, you live below, don't you?' said Mr. Budd. 'You get along. I wish I could go home, too, but I shall be here for a good while yet.'

'If there's anything I can do just let me know,' said Smedhurst and left them.

Mr. Budd stood looking down at the dead taxi-driver in silence, pinching his fat chin between a finger and thumb. His brows were drawn together and his lips pursed. Sergeant Leek leant against the wall and closed his eyes. The superintendent was still standing there when Doctor Salisbury came back.

'Strangled,' he said bluntly. 'Drugged up to the eyes, too. Let's have a look at this chap.'

He knelt down beside the body.

'Be careful how you remove the knife,' grunted Mr. Budd. 'Draw it out by the guard an' give it to Leek.'

'All right, don't fuss!' said the divisional-surgeon. 'Done these jobs before, you know.'

At that moment, Gordon and John Stayner came down from above. The elder man was in a state of suppressed excitement.

'I say,' he said, 'there's something very strange about this night's business . . . '

'You surprise me!' said Mr. Budd sarcastically. 'I thought murder was very ordinary.'

'I'm not referring to that,' said Stayner hastily. 'I mean about my daughter — I've just been on the telephone to her friend — she's not ill. She never telephoned Margaret at all.'

Mr. Budd became suddenly interested.

'Oh,' he murmured softly. 'So she didn't, didn't she?'

'The message was a fake,' said Gordon.

'Now that's very interestin' an' peculiar,' said the superintendent, pulling at his nose gently. 'Very interestin' indeed.'

'They wanted her out of the way in case she saw too much,' suggested Stayner, but Mr. Budd shook his head.

'This murder wasn't planned,' he said. 'It was carried out hastily on the spur of the moment because this feller, Jameson, knew somethin' an' he had to be silenced — like the taxi-driver. It was all played off the cuff. No, there was some other reason for gettin' Miss Stayner out of the way.'

There was a muffled thud and a bright flash from the sitting-room.

'What's that?' asked the startled Gordon.

'Takin' photographs,' answered Mr. Budd absently. 'Just a matter of routine. We shan't catch Mister Big that way . . . Well, doctor?'

The divisional-surgeon had risen to his feet.

'The man was stabbed with a thin-bladed knife. It pierced the heart and the blow was struck with considerable force. He died instantly. That's as much as I can tell you until after the P.M.' He brushed the knees of his trousers.

'I thought he was strangled?' began Gordon.

'We're talkin' about the taxi-driver,' explained Mr. Budd wearily. 'There have been two killin's here tonight.'

Gordon Trent stared at him and then he saw the body by the chair.

'Good God, this is awful,' he muttered.

'I suppose you didn't see anythin' when you came out with Miss Stayner?' asked Mr. Budd.

Gordon shook his head.

'No, I didn't.'

'Did you, sir?' Mr. Budd turned to Stayner.

'No, I saw him sitting there but he looked as if he'd fallen asleep,' answered the M.P.

'It was a deeper sleep than he'd ever been in before,' grunted the superintendent. 'I shall be leavin' an officer here in charge but he won't interfere with you, Mr. Trent.'

'What are you going to do?' asked Gordon.

'I'm goin' back to the Yard,' said Mr. Budd.

'What do we do now?' asked the sleepy-eyed sergeant when they finally left the flats and emerged into Victoria Street.

'I'm goin' to do a lot of thinkin',' replied his superior.

'Then you won't want me, will you?' said Leek with unconscious humour.

'Thinkin' isn't your strong point,' agreed Mr. Budd. 'But I shall want you all the same.'

Leek who had had visions of a

51

comfortable bed and a long sleep sighed unhappily.

When they reached the stout superintendent's office Mr. Budd settled himself in the padded chair behind his desk and lit one of his black, evil-smelling cigars. Leaning back with closed eyes, his hands clasped across his capacious stomach, he sat motionless, the ash from his cigar dropping unheeded down his waistcoat.

Dawn was breaking greyly and the stub of the cigar, long since cold, still protruded from his lips, when he roused himself and brought his fist down with a bang on the desk.

'Got it!' he exclaimed triumphantly.

Sergeant Leek, fast asleep in a corner with his head against the wall, heard the noise, and dreaming that Mr. Budd had shot himself, smiled happily.

6

Gordon Trent did not go to bed at all that night. After the departure of Mr. Budd and Leek, he and Stayner went up to the latter's flat. A uniformed constable had arrived in answer to Mr. Budd's telephoned orders, and he made himself comfortable after the two bodies had been removed, in the sitting-room. Gordon, worried about Margaret, welcomed her father's invitation to come up for a drink.

After he had looked in to assure himself that the girl was sleeping peacefully, Stayner came back and poured out two Johnnie Walkers, gave one to Gordon, and drank the other himself almost at a gulp.

'By Jove, I needed that!' he declared pouring out another. 'I don't like this business at all. I don't mean those two murders, they're dreadful, of course, I mean this bogus telephone call.' He helped himself to a little water. 'Why should anyone want to get Margaret away?'

'I don't know,' said Gordon. 'It couldn't have had anything to do with the murders, could it? Budd doesn't think it had.'

'He didn't impress me as being very bright,' said Stayner, falling into the misconception that most people who didn't know the stout superintendent intimately usually did. 'I'm very worried about this fake call. If it happened once it might happen again . . . '

'She wouldn't take any notice a second time,' said Gordon.

'It may not be the same sort of thing a second time,' said the M.P. gravely. 'I wish I could think of a reason.'

But Gordon couldn't help him. He was as much puzzled as the other. Somehow or other, he thought that it was rather a lucky thing for Margaret that the accident had happened. What would have waited for her if she had completed her journey? Would she have merely found out that it was only a trick or would there have been a more sinister ending?

He mentioned this to Stayner and the M.P. nodded.

'That's what I've been wondering,' he said seriously.

It was nearly five when Gordon got back to his own flat to find the constable asleep in the easy chair. The man woke up as he entered and Trent asked him if he'd like a cup of coffee. The constable was enthusiastic and Gordon went into the kitchen to make it. He was in the midst of this when the front-door bell rang.

Wondering who it could be at that early hour, and concluding that it was probably the police, Gordon was going to see when he heard the constable forestall him.

A high-pitched voice inquired 'if Mr. Trent was in' and Gordon almost ran out into the hall. A tall, rather gangling figure was standing at the open front door. The face of this individual broke into a wide grin as he caught sight of Gordon.

'Hello, can I come in?' he called.

'Of course,' said Gordon. 'I'm just making some coffee.'

'Good!' The newcomer threw his hat on the hall table revealing a mass of flaming red hair. 'How did you know I was coming?'

'I didn't, you ass!' said Gordon. 'I was making it for myself and the constable.'

'I see,' the red-haired young man grinned. 'No V.I.P. treatment. Glad I didn't have to wake you up. Been having a bit of a beano here, haven't you? Old Pillbox sent me to gather all the gory details.'

'I'm glad he sent you, Colin,' said Gordon. Old Pillbox was the name by which Mr. Pillbeam, the night news editor of the *Post-Bulletin* was known to his staff.

'Who else could they send with the same amount of genius!' remarked Colin Dugan. 'I am the greatest crime reporter in Fleet Street!'

'And the most modest obviously,' said Gordon. 'Go into the sitting-room and I'll fetch the coffee.'

He hurried back to the kitchen just in time to stop the percolator boiling over. Colin and he were great friends. They had first met during Gordon's free-lance reporting days, and remained friends ever since, though they seldom met.

Dugan was lank and tall and raw-boned with a face that kindly people called 'rugged,' and heavily peppered with freckles. His favourite attire were a pair of narrow, very creased flannel trousers and a suede jacket. A duffle-coat which he wore on wet or cold days completed the ensemble. He usually wore a tweed hat that looked too small for him perched on his flaming hair, and he owned a scooter which looked in imminent danger of falling to pieces. He had once, and only once, persuaded Gordon to ride on the pillion, and his friend was convinced that only a beneficent providence had allowed him to survive the ordeal.

'Now,' said Dugan when Gordon brought in the coffee, 'tell me about the excitement.'

'I'll tell you as much as I know,' said Gordon. He lit a cigarette and pushed the box across to his friend. 'And that isn't much.'

The constable had discreetly retired with his coffee to the kitchen so he was able to speak quite freely. Colin listened without comment until he had finished, then he whistled softly.

'Well, you certainly had the lot, didn't you?' he remarked. 'Why do you think these two chaps were killed?'

Trent took a gulp of coffee before he answered.

'It's obvious, isn't it? Poor Jameson knew something about this man, Mister Big, and so did the taxi-driver. They were killed to shut 'em up.'

Colin helped himself to a cigarette and frowned at it.

'H'm!' he grunted non-committally. 'How d'you suppose Jameson got in that condition?'

Gordon shrugged his shoulders.

'Your guess is as good as mine,' he answered. 'I can't account for it.'

'It's a bit queer that he should've turned up suddenly like that after such a long time. It strikes me as very curious. He disappears for five years and then turns up out of the blue looking like a tramp an' full of drugs. How did he know where to find you?'

'That's easy,' replied Gordon. 'I was

living here when he went to West Berlin. He wrote once to this address.'

'You say there was absolutely nothing in his pockets — nothing at all?'

'That's right.'

'How do you account for it?'

'I can't.'

'There's one explanation,' said Colin thoughtfully.

'What?'

'That for some time before he came to see you, he was kept a prisoner somewhere . . . '

'By the man they call Mister Big?'

'Seems reasonable. If this fellow had discovered who he was . . . '

'Why keep him prisoner?' interrupted Gordon. 'It would've been easier to kill him — and safer.'

'There's a point there,' agreed Colin. 'I can't suggest a reason off-hand.' He ran a bony hand through his hair. 'This girl,' he went on. 'How does she come into it?

'I don't know that she does come into it,' said Gordon. 'I don't see how she can . . . '

'Oh, now, come off it!' expostulated

Colin. 'You're not going to tell me that that telephone call was just a coincidence?'

'I don't see that it could have been anything else.'

'I distrust that kind of coincidence,' grunted the reporter. 'It fits too well.'

'It's certainly queer . . . '

'Very! I'd like to know what would have happened if she hadn't had that accident.'

'Presumably, she'd have gone on to her friend's house and found that the whole thing was a hoax,' said Gordon. 'Like some more coffee?'

Colin shook his head.

'I wonder if that's all that would have happened?' he said.

He uncoiled himself and got up, went over to the window, and tapped gently on the glass. Then he swung round quickly.

'Look here,' he said. 'Are you busy?'

'Not very.' Gordon looked at him in surprise. 'Why?'

Colin came back to the settee.

'I shall get the job of 'covering' this for the *Bulletin*,' he explained. 'We've been interested in the activities of this Big man for a long time. Suppose you and I join forces and see what we can discover between us?'

Trent looked a little dubious.

'I don't know much about this sort of thing,' he began, but Colin interrupted him.

'You don't have to,' he said. 'All you've got to do is use your common sense. If we could find this man, Mister Big, it 'ud be a big scoop for the paper — no joke intended, by the way!'

'How d'you propose to set about it?'

'Well, we know two things about him which we didn't know before,' answered Dugan. 'Both are suggestive and might help.'

'What do you mean? What two things?'

'The taxi-driver recognised him, didn't he? That's why he was killed. So he's fairly well known in this district. Right?'

'Go on.'

'That's one. The other is that the phone message that sent this girl on a false errand was supposed to come from a great friend of hers. If it was sent by Mister Big . . . '

'We don't know that it was . . . '

'I said 'if,'' continued Colin. 'Don't interrupt! If it came from Mister Big he must have a good knowledge of the Stayners' private affairs to know that the girl had a friend named Eileen. See what I mean?'

'I hear what you say,' said Gordon cautiously. 'We've no proof that the telephone message had anything to do with the rest of it, have we?

'If it was just a joke,' said Colin, 'we must find the joker.' He flicked the ash from his cigarette on to the floor. 'Who did you say was in charge of the case?'

'A big, fat chap. Looks as if he was half asleep all the time . . . '

'Budd!' exclaimed Colin. 'Don't you be misled by that sleepy stuff. It's all bunk! I'm going back to the office now. I'll come back again in about an hour. Have some breakfast ready and then we'll pop over to the Yard and see Budd. O.K.?'

'I suppose so,' agreed Gordon reluctantly. 'Can't you get your own breakfast?'

'Always be hospitable, old boy. That's the thing to win friends and popularity!'

He went over to the door. 'Toast and marmalade'll do,' he said and departed.

Gordon decided that he could do with a spot of sleep. He didn't fancy going to bed so he made himself as comfortable as he could on the settee and almost instantly fell asleep.

When he woke up it was just on seven o'clock. He shaved, had a bath, and felt better. The daily woman who 'did' for him had not yet put in an appearance. She wasn't supposed to come before eight and since Colin might come back at any moment, Gordon decided to get the breakfast he had demanded.

He found some eggs and some bacon and he was cooking these when Colin re-appeared.

'That smells good!' he greeted, following Gordon back to the kitchen. 'I'm as hungry as a starving tramp!'

'You asked for toast,' retorted Gordon maliciously. 'The eggs and bacon are for me!'

'Men have died for less than that!' cried Colin. 'If you're going to hog all the eggs and bacon . . .'

'Don't get all worked up, there's plenty for both of us,' said Gordon. 'Here, get hold of a tray and make yourself useful.'

Presently they sat down to breakfast and invited the constable to join them, which he did with alacrity. They were just finishing when the cleaning woman arrived. She gaped at the sight of the policeman, and gaped even wider when Gordon explained why he was there. They left her to clear away the remains, assisted by the constable, and went to seek out Mr. Budd at the Yard.

They found him seated behind his desk, more sleepy-eyed than ever.

'So you're in this business, are you?' he grunted when Colin was shown in. 'I hope you enjoy it! Goin' to work together, are you? That'll be nice an' frien'ly. Come to pump me, have you?'

Colin grinned.

'If you've anything fresh,' he said.

'Well, I have,' said Mr. Budd grimly. 'But it's not for publication — understand?'

'You know me,' said Colin. 'Close as an oyster, I am.'

'Take a look at that!' growled the super-intendent. He stretched out a chubby hand and picked up a slip of paper which he flicked across the desk. Colin glanced at it and his face was suddenly serious.

Keep out of my business. This is a warning. I shall not repeat it. Don't force me to treat you like the taxi-driver.

There was no signature but they all knew who had sent it.

'When did you get this?' asked Colin. 'By this morning's post?'

'No. I found it in my overcoat pocket half an hour ago. Good staff work, eh?'

Mr. Budd took a cigar out of his pocket, looked at it, and put it back again.

'What are you going to do about it?' asked Gordon.

Mr. Budd shrugged his wide shoulders.

'Nothin',' he answered, and yawned. 'A lot of people have sent me warnin's, but I'm still alive an' kickin' — which is more than some of them are,' he added.

'This chap doesn't utter idle threats,' said Colin. 'You're going to find life full

65

of possibilities during the next few days.'

Mr. Budd took out the cigar again, sniffed it and rolled it gently between his fingers.

'Life is always full of possibilities,' he remarked sententiously. 'I'm not under-rating this warnin'. I know just how dangerous this feller is. But I'm not exactly a Sunday school treat myself, you know!'

The sleepy eyes had gone suddenly hard and there was an edge to the usual drawling voice. Gordon Trent sensing the steel behind that lethargic exterior was inclined to agree with him.

7

Half-way down Upper Thames Street, that unsalubrious and malodorous thoroughfare that runs parallel with the river, stands a ramshackle building that looks in imminent danger of falling down.

Not that this description would be sufficient on its own to distinguish it from its immediate neighbours, for the buildings in this district are pretty much the same.

This particular building is, however, rather more smoke-grimed and mean-looking than its fellows. Its narrow entrance with the dirty stone steps, dark and forbidding even on the brightest day, is not inviting, but this is a business area where people care little for outward appearances.

A list of names painted in dingy black lettering on an equally dingy grey wall, testified that a number of firms used this unpleasant building as a place of business. This wall had once been white, but age and dirt and smoke had combined to reduce it over the years to a uniform grey that made it difficult to decipher the names of the tenants that were displayed on its flaking surface.

There was one, however, that appeared to be a little fresher than the others. 'A. Jacobs. Third Floor' was obviously of more recent origin.

Dusk was falling on the evening following the murders in Gordon Trent's flat, and the work of the day had long since ceased, for the denizens of Upper Thames Street begin early and finish early, when a man in a dirty raincoat turned into the entrance to the flight of steps that lead down from London Bridge, and began to walk quickly along the narrow and almost deserted street.

He wore his hat pulled down low over his eyes so that it was difficult to distinguish his face. He walked with the assured step of one who is very familiar with the ground he traversed, and at last he came to the entrance of the building which housed Mr. A. Jacobs of unmentioned occupation.

He turned into the dark entry and mounted the grimy stair to the third floor. A dirt-encrusted window faced him on the landing, and on his right a single door, on which the name of Mr. Jacobs had been repeated in letters of a dubious whiteness.

The man in the raincoat stopped outside this door and pressed a small bell-push in the door frame. He pressed it three times quickly, paused, and then gave a long ring. There was no sound from within of a bell but he wasn't surprised at this because he knew that the bell had been replaced by a soft-toned buzzer that could not be heard from outside.

There was a slight interval after he had removed his finger from the push, and then with a faint click, the door opened an inch.

The visitor pushed it wider and stepped into the darkness beyond. The electrically controlled door closed behind him.

For a moment he stood in complete darkness and then a dim bulb glowed in the ceiling. He was in a small room, divided in half by a counter that stretched from wall to wall with a flap in the middle. An ancient filing cabinet stood in one corner and behind the counter was a table with a chair, both old and almost falling to pieces.

The window was shuttered and over the shutters had been pasted sheets of brown paper that sealed it completely. The room was empty, but lifting the counter-flap, the man in the raincoat crossed the bare, uncarpeted floor to a door that faced the one by which he had entered. Again he pressed a small bell-push — two long presses followed by one short this time — and again there was a click and the door swung open.

'Come in, Sullivan.' The voice came out of the darkness, metallic, toneless, almost inhuman.

Sullivan entered. The door closed at once and clicked shut. There was no illumination here at first. Then a very dim light glowed from the ceiling, dimmer than the one in the outer office. This room, too, was empty, but Sullivan seemed to find nothing unusual in this.

He walked over to a small table set against the wall and sat down in the chair in front of it.

He waited and presently part of the wall above the table slid back. An aperture less than two feet square and covered with a screen of fine wire gauze was revealed. Beyond the gauze was nothing, only darkness.

'You failed last night, Sullivan,' said the voice that had spoken before, unnatural and inhuman.

'Yes,' answered Sullivan. 'It wasn't our fault. The girl never turned up.'

'Her taxi met with an accident. No blame attaches to you or Brooks. Another attempt must be made — at once.'

'We can't use the same stunt again,' began Sullivan, but the emotionless voice interrupted him.

'I'm not suggesting that you should,' it said. 'You, Brooks, and Cameron must keep Wellington Mansions under close watch. Use the taxi and the van and take it in turns. The girl doesn't often go out after dark without someone with her, but there will be an opportunity. You must get her, and get her soon.'

'It's goin' to be difficult,' said Sullivan. 'We don't know what she looks like. It was different last night, we knew she was comin' . . . '

'She's tall, slim build, and fair-haired. She wears a grey squirrel coat or if it's wet a pink raincoat. She's the only girl like that in the flats. The only other girl there is small and dark.'

'We'll do our best,' said Sullivan.

'I don't want your best — I want a certainty,' snapped the disembodied voice. 'That girl's got to be in my hands by the end of next week at the latest. Don't make any mistake, Sullivan!'

There was menace in the voice, and Sullivan gave a little shiver.

'It'll be done,' he said. 'Is there anything else?'

'Yes. Tomorrow morning a man called William Sutton is to be released from Norwich Prison. He must not reach London alive. Get somebody you can rely on. There's five hundred pounds for the man who does the job.'

'I'll get Al Davis. For five hundred quid

he'd shoot his own mother! What's the idea of bumpin' off this feller, Sutton?'

'That's my business,' answered the voice. 'You do as you're told and don't get curious. It's a bad habit. Cure it!'

'I'm sorry,' muttered Sullivan.

'There is another thing,' went on the voice. 'Who was responsible for letting the man, Jameson, get away? It was very nearly disastrous.'

'It was Willings. I was after the girl. I couldn't be in two places at once . . . '

'I don't want excuses! You should have seen that the man who was guarding Jameson was reliable. Now, listen carefully. There is a man, Superintendent Budd. I want him disposed of. I'll tell you how it is to be done. This is the plan. You'll need to use Charley . . . '

'That little 'dip,'' broke in Sullivan.

'Don't interrupt. I told you to listen!'

Sullivan listened, while the voice outlined the plan for the disposal of Mr. Budd.

'That's clever,' he said when the voice ceased.

'You must attend to the girl and Sutton

first. They are priority. Now, you'll find your usual payment in the drawer of the table. Be here at the same time the day after tomorrow. And don't fail to carry out your instructions this time!'

The panel in the wall slid back covering the aperture. The interview was over.

Sullivan got up and opened the narrow drawer in the table. He took out a thin packet of notes which he put in his pocket. Going out into the other office he touched the bell-push. The door of the inner room which he had just left closed with a sharp click. He repeated this procedure with the outer door of the other office. Immediately the light went out and that door, too, closed behind him.

Mr. A. Jacobs' business was over.

Sullivan felt his way down the dark stairway and out into Upper Thames Street. He lit a cigarette and walked quickly away.

Behind him shuffled an ill-clad figure, glancing apprehensively about him as he followed the man in front. And there was reason for his apprehension.

Gabby Smith had learned something that night that would make him a very welcome visitor at the narrow door where certain men pass into Scotland Yard under cover of darkness — always provided that he could reach his destination alive.

8

Sergeant Leek gazed mournfully at the melancholy reflection of his long, thin face in the mirror of his dressing-table. With a sigh he patted his black bow-tie into position, adjusted the cuffs of his soft dress-shirt, and picked up the dinner-jacket that lay ready on a convenient chair.

His lank figure looked a little peculiar in the dinner-suit, rather like a half-starved crow, but he seemed fairly satisfied. He wondered what Mr. Budd would say if he could see him now? Something rude most likely. Oh, well, he didn't care! He was going to enjoy himself! This was the proper way to live he decided. It is doubtful if Mr. Budd would have survived the shock of his usually seedy and weary subordinate, but at that moment Mr. Budd was entirely occupied speculating on the approaching interview with Gabby Smith to worry about the lean sergeant. In point of fact he had forgotten that he existed!

Except for the habitual melancholy of his expression which nothing could alter, Leek looked as happy as it was possible for him to be. He put on his overcoat, remembered the white silk scarf, and put that on too, pulling the collar of the coat over it. Locking the door of his room, he walked down the stairs into the street.

The Kennington Road does not cater for gentlemen in evening dress. They are rare and far between in this district. Several people turned to look at the tall, thin figure in black as it passed and decided that it must be an undertaker going on his lawful occasions.

A taxi came along in the direction of Westminster and Leek hailed it. He gave the driver a brief direction and was driven rapidly away.

Outside a club in Regent Street he alighted, paid off the taxi, and went into the vestibule. By what means he gained admittance was known only to himself, but after a few words with the fat manager, who was also the owner, he was bowed down a flight of steps in the converted cellars which formed the premises called the Silver Shoe.

Why it was called the Silver Shoe was known only to the people who named it. Perhaps some childish recollection of Cinderella had influenced them. Certainly there was nothing childish about the Silver Shoe except the clientele who paid exorbitant prices for inferior food, inferior drink, and inferior entertainment.

The head waiter conducted Leek to a vacant table at one corner of the small dance floor. The band had just finished playing the latest hit by the Insects, a captivating little ditty called 'Baby, Please put the Cat Out Instead of Me' and the dancers had already returned to their various tables. The party of three who sat in one of the alcoves had an uninterrupted view of the arrival of the sergeant.

'Look, surely that's the sergeant who came with Superintendent Budd to my flat?' said Gordon Trent, turning to John Stayner in astonishment.

The M.P. looked over to where Leek was settling himself in his chair.

'Yes, I think it is,' he replied. 'What's he doing here, do you imagine?'

'I hope it isn't a raid,' said Gordon. He looked at the girl beside him. 'I should hate to let you in for that.'

'I shouldn't mind,' she said. 'But it would look rather bad for father. M.P.s have to mind their reputations.'

Except for a slight cut on one cheek and a large bruise on her left arm she had quite recovered from the accident of the previous night. It had been at her suggestion that they had come to the Silver Shoe. She had never been to a night club and although they both tried to dissuade her, she insisted that that was where she wanted to go, so they capitulated.

Gordon looked carefully around. The waiters were going about their duties unperturbed. They must have known that Leek was a police officer, at least the management must. They know all of them by sight, and they didn't seem in the least worried.

He mentioned this to the other two.

'Perhaps he's just enjoying himself,'

said Margaret. 'I suppose he can when he's off duty, if he wants to?'

'He doesn't look as if he were enjoying himself,' remarked Stayner. 'What's that he's ordered?'

They watched with interest. A waiter brought a gold-topped bottle to Leek's table.

'Champagne at five pounds a bottle!' breathed Gordon. 'He's doing himself well. It looks decidedly fishy to me! They don't pay police officers as well as that.'

Fishy or otherwise the champagne was opened and the foaming contents creamed into the glass at Leek's elbow. Consulting the menu, the sergeant gave an order and proceeded to sip his champagne.

'He doesn't look as if he liked it,' said the girl.

'They buy the bottles, empty, from reputable hotels and restaurants from the waiters, it's quite a business. Then they fill 'em with inferior champagne, put in a fresh cork and cover it with gold foil, and — voila! A bottle of champagne bearing a famous name and vintage.'

'But that's fraud!' exclaimed the girl.

'Can't they be stopped?'

'Who's going to give 'em away?' asked Gordon. 'My word! Caviare! I say he's going strong!'

The band began another number and Gordon looked at Margaret. She nodded and they got up and joined the other dancers on the floor.

When the band-leader in a nasal voice had several times assured everybody 'It was Nobody's Fault but My Own' the band stopped playing and they rejoined John Stayner.

Leek was no longer alone, but had been joined by a stout, flashy looking man. In the intervals of eating his caviare, Leek was listening to what he was saying. He had apparently ordered a second glass for his companion who gulped it noisily between sentences. The sergeant waited until he stopped and then he nodded. The stout man took something from his pocket and slid it across the table. Leek took it and slipped it into his jacket pocket. The stout man smiled. Leek refilled his glass and the stout man took a tremendous gulp.

When Gordon and the other two took their leave Leek and the stout man were still talking . . .

It was a fine night and the air smelt cool and sweet after the stuffy, smoke and perfume-laden atmosphere of the club, and they declined the taxi that swerved into the kerb, and decided to walk.

'I enjoyed myself thoroughly,' declared Margaret, 'but I don't think I should like a sustained course of night club life.'

Gordon laughed.

'They are rather an acquired taste,' he said.

'That police sergeant seems to have acquired the taste pretty well,' remarked Stayner dryly.

'It looks queer to me,' said Gordon. 'I think it ought to be brought to the notice of his superiors . . .'

'Oh, why?' protested Margaret. 'It might get him into trouble. Let the poor man amuse himself that way if he wants to.'

'Poor men don't amuse themselves at places like the Silver Shoe,' replied Gordon truthfully. 'However, I suppose it's really no concern of ours.'

They began to chat about other things until they crossed the broad space by the Houses of Parliament which narrows into Victoria Street.

'Eileen's coming to tea tomorrow,' said Margaret after a short silence.

'You mean today,' corrected Stayner with a smile.

'Yes, I suppose I do,' agreed the girl. 'Why don't you come too and meet her, Mr. Trent?'

'I'd like to,' said Gordon.

The street was deserted, but as they neared the entrance to Wellington Mansions, Gordon saw the figure of a man come out of a dark doorway further along and walk slowly towards them.

He appeared to be a rather shabbily dressed individual in an old raincoat. His chin was covered with a stubble of beard and he wore no hat. Gordon glanced at him casually as he passed and took no further notice until they had almost reached the entrance to the flats. Then some instinct, a warning of approaching danger, made him swing round suddenly.

He was only just in time!

The shabby stranger had doubled back and was in the act of lunging at John Stayner's back with something that glittered in the street lamps.

Gordon sprang forward and knocked up his arm. The man gave a grunt of pain and the long-bladed knife flew from his hand and clattered on the pavement.

Trent made a grab at the attacker's shoulder, and received a blow on the chin that sent him staggering against the M.P. Before he could recover his balance, the shabby man had taken to his heels and was flying down the street.

'That was a close call!' panted Gordon. 'He nearly got you!'

John Stayner said nothing, but he had gone white to the lips and there was a look of fear in his eyes.

9

The attack on Stayner kept Gordon awake half the night. It was not until the very early hours that he finally fell asleep and by then he had made up his mind.

In spite of the fact that the M.P. had denied all knowledge of the shabby stranger, Gordon decided to go round to the Yard and tell Mr. Budd about it.

He found the stout superintendent sitting behind his big desk, a weary and rather disgruntled man. Nothing had happened to help him at all in his investigations and he was suffering from that most nerve-racking of all nervous complaints, frustration.

He listened attentively to Gordon's story, put a question now and again, and finally shook his head.

'Interestin' — very interestin',' he remarked. 'An' that's even more interestin'.' He cocked a sleepy eye at the knife which lay before him. Gordon had picked it up and brought it with him. 'That's Government property,' he went on. 'See that broad arrow cut into the handle. How did he get hold of it, eh? Must've picked it up somewhere. Anythin' else you can tell me about him?'

'Nothing more than I've already told you.'

Mr. Budd sighed.

'You think Stayner knew this feller?' he asked.

'Well,' answered Gordon cautiously, 'I won't go so far as that but I noticed a very peculiar look in his eyes . . . '

'If some lunatic had nearly stuck a knife in my back,' he said, 'you'd have noticed a very peculiar look in *my* eyes! I can't think of anythin' more likely to make me look peculiar.'

'You know very well what I mean,' said Gordon. 'It was a queer look — almost fear.'

'You think that he knew the reason why this chap was tryin' to knife him?'

'Yes, I do.'

'Then why keep it a secret?' demanded Mr. Budd.

'I don't know, but he definitely didn't

want to discuss it,' said Trent.

'H'm! Maybe I'll have a word with him about it,' said the stout superintendent. 'I'm very glad you came along an' told me. If we lay our hands on the feller I'll get you to identify him.'

Gordon got up to leave. At the door he stopped and hesitated.

'There's something else you ought to know,' he said.

Mr. Budd looked at him and the sleepy expression had gone from his eyes.

'Yes?' he enquired.

'I saw your sergeant last night — at the Silver Shoe.' Gordon told him what he had seen and Mr. Budd listened without comment until he had finished.

'The Silver Shoe, eh?' he remarked. 'Gone gay? Well, well, fancy that now! Fancy Leek turnin' into a bright young thing. I shouldn't have thought he could've kept awake long enough!'

'I thought at first he might have been on duty . . . '

'Just innocent amusement, Mr. Trent,' murmured Mr. Budd gently. 'Just innocent amusement.'

He sank back comfortably in his chair, and at that moment a constable entered to announce that Colin Dugan wished to see him.

'No rest for the wicked,' grumbled Mr. Budd. 'Shoot him in.'

'I wonder what he wants?' said Gordon.

'Tryin' to pick my brains,' retorted the big man.

Colin came in briskly and looked rather surprised to see his friend.

'Hello!' he exclaimed. 'What are you doing here? Anything fresh?'

'What's brought you along so early?' demanded Mr. Budd before Trent could answer. 'Got somethin' to tell me?'

Colin grinned and shook his head.

'I was hoping you might have something to tell *me*,' he answered.

'What did I tell you?' Mr. Budd made a grimace at Gordon. 'The day I learn anythin' from a reporter will give me such a shock I'll probably never recover.'

Colin's sharp eyes had spotted the knife on the desk.

'Hello,' he cried. 'What's that?'

'That very nearly found a home in John Stayner's back last night,' retorted Mr. Budd. 'You can keep this to yourself. I don't want it broadcast through that rag of yours.'

'All right. Go ahead.'

Mr. Budd repeated the story that Gordon had told him.

'What do you make of that?' he asked.

Colin Dugan shook his head.

'Nothing! Jolly queer, isn't it?'

'You're a fat lot of help!' growled Mr. Budd.

'Where's the connection between all these various events?' frowned the reporter. 'There must be one. They can't be isolated . . .'

'I agree with you,' said Mr. Budd. 'But I'm hanged if I can puzzle out what it is. I can't see what reason there was for getting that girl out of the way. Jameson didn't call to see her. He wasn't even in the same flat.'

'I still think that was somebody's idea of a joke,' said Gordon.

'Was that someone's idea of a joke too?' said Mr. Budd pointing at the knife.

'There was no joke about that,' answered Trent seriously. 'If I hadn't been there, Stayner wouldn't be alive now.'

'You say the attack didn't surprise him?' asked Colin.

'Not exactly. I got the impression that it didn't. But I may have been wrong.'

'There are a lot of these half-baked lunatics goin' around these days,' growled the superintendent. 'Don't know what's come over most people these days. We never used to get such a lot of violence . . . '

'You dry nurse 'em, don't you?' said Colin. 'They kick some poor devil half to death and what happens? They get let off with a fine and told not to do it again. And some idiot talks a lot of rubbish about being mixed up and frustration complex and all the modern nonsense. Bring back the cat for violence. I'll bet you it 'ud stop in next to no time. These hooligans only understand one thing — physical pain.'

Mr. Budd nodded slowly.

'You're quite right, of course,' he said. 'But you can't go back to flogging,' protested Gordon. 'This is a civilised age . . . '

Colin uttered a hoot of derision.

'Civilised, my foot!' he cried. 'There never was an age when cruelty was so rampant. Most of the younger generation are a lot of sadists, both girls and boys. Belsen would've given them a great kick. They have no morals, no standards of behaviour, and precious few brains. The wonder to me is that everybody is so complacent about it. Surely there must be somebody who has brains enough to realise that unless very drastic steps are taken, and soon, the menace of these thugs will swamp the country.'

'We can't do anythin',' said Mr. Budd. 'I believe you're right, but the problem must be tackled at the highest level. The trouble is that the people in power don't know a thing about it. They don't come into contact with violence themselves. All they do is appoint a lot of half-baked committees to prepare a report. Has a committee ever done any good? Of course not! They spend years arguing and discussing and finish where they began.'

He shrugged his shoulders. 'Let's get back to the job in hand. I've cabled the West German police an' asked 'em to trace up Jameson's movements from the time he went there five years ago. If we can find out what happened to him, who he was in contact with from the time he went there to the time he turned up at your flat, it might give us a line to somethin'.'

'It would help a great deal more if you could find out where he came *from* to Trent's flat,' said Colin. 'That would help you a great deal more.'

Mr. Budd regarded him across the desk with eyes that had grown thoughtful.

'Explain what you mean by that?' he said.

'Colin thinks he was kept a prisoner somewhere,' put in Gordon.

'I suppose you noticed the mark on his ankles,' said Mr. Budd. 'I had the same idea, you know. He escaped an' naturally made his way to his friend's address. That it?'

Colin made a grimace.

'You don't miss much,' he commented.

'It's my job not to miss anythin',' said Mr. Budd. 'I don't always live up to that, but I try. Why should Jameson have been kept prisoner?'

'Because he knew something about Mister Big?' suggested Gordon.

'Meanin' that it was the Big Feller who was keepin' him prisoner?' said the superintendent.

'Yes.'

'Well, we shall see.' Mr. Budd yawned and stretched himself. 'Now, I've got a lot to do so you'd better clear out. We shan't catch this feller by sittin' here talkin'.'

When they had gone, he sat for a moment or two staring at the ceiling, then he pulled the house telephone nearer and gave an extension number to the switchboard. When he was connected, he said:

'I want a man to trail Sergeant Leek day and night. He's not to be lost sight of for a single instant. He's not to know that he's being tailed. Have him picked up when he leaves here. That's all.'

He put down the receiver, took out and lit one of his black cigars, and leaned back in his chair with a sigh.

'You'd better go carefully, Leek, my friend,' he murmured softly to himself. 'If you don't you're goin' to get yourself in trouble — bad trouble!'

10

The man seated in the taxi, drawn up at the kerb within sight of the entrance to Wellington Mansions, lit a cigarette from the stub of the one he had just finished, threw the stub out of the window, and huddled back in his seat with a grunt of utter boredom.

Mr. Sullivan was fed up. For two hours he had been watching the flats from various parts of the street in the hope that the girl he was waiting for would come out. But so far he hadn't caught a glimpse of her. To add to the dreariness of his vigil, it had started to rain.

It had been the same on the previous night. After a long and unprofitable time spent in watching the flats he had had the doubtful satisfaction of seeing the girl leave in the company of two men and drive off in a taxi.

He had followed them to the Silver Shoe and had decided to call it a day. It wasn't much use waiting. They would all come home together and there wouldn't be any chance of getting the girl alone.

It looked as if he was going to draw another blank. He swore softly. Didn't the girl ever go out on her own? He had to make his report to the Big Man on the following day and he already had one failure to his credit which disturbed him quite a lot.

He had sent Al Davis to pick up William Sutton from the prison and that enterprising gunman had telephoned to say that William Sutton had been released four days previously.

Mister Big must have muddled the date somehow, but that didn't make Sullivan feel any the less uneasy. He would get the full force of the other's temper.

If this could be diluted by getting hold of the girl, he could face the interview on the following night with much greater confidence. But if he had to report that a failure too . . .

He caught his breath suddenly and leaning forward pulled back the sliding window to the driver's seat.

'There she is!' he said excitedly to the man in the driving seat. 'That girl in the pink raincoat who has just come out. She's looking for a taxi, too! Jump to it, man!'

He slid the window back and pressed back into his corner as the cab moved forward and approached the girl who had just come out of the flats and was standing undecidedly on the edge of the pavement looking about.

'Taxi, miss?' called the driver as the cab swerved towards her.

'Yes — take me to Victoria Station,' she said and got in. The cab started with a jerk, and then she saw the man crouching in the corner and opened her lips to give a cry of alarm. But Sullivan was prepared. The needle of the syringe he held in his hand stabbed into her arm. She tried to struggle but the drug took effect almost at once and she suddenly went limp.

Sullivan put her down on the seat and slid back the window.

'She's off!' he said. 'You can drive to Upper Thames Street.'

The taxi swung into a side street,

turned into another, and headed for the city. It was that blank period between the theatre crowds going in and coming out when the traffic is least congested, and they made good progress. Less than half an hour after they had left Victoria Street, the cab pulled up at the entrance to a narrow alley in Upper Thames Street.

Sullivan got out quickly, looked round to assure himself that the place was deserted, and lifted out the girl. The cab drove off immediately and he carried the girl into the dark mouth of the alleyway.

Carrying his burden easily, Sullivan walked rapidly along the narrow passage — which was only a space between the high walls of two warehouses — until he came to a wooden door at the end. Putting the girl down for a moment he searched in his pocket, found a key, and unlocked the door. Pushing it open, he picked up the girl, entered, and closed the door behind him.

The darkness was intense but he fumbled along the wall until he found a light switch. A glimmer of yellow light came on in a dirty bulb above his head. He was in a passage that ended in another door. Unlocking this, too, he found himself in a large room that was apparently part of the lower floor of the warehouse. A rough partition a few feet higher than his head divided it from the rest of the building.

Sullivan put the girl down, wiped the perspiration from his face, and went back through the passage and relocked the outer door. Coming back he looked at his watch and went over to a small cupboard. He opened it disclosing a telephone.

Lifting the receiver he listened. There was a click and a voice said : 'Yes. Who is that?'

'Sullivan,' answered Sullivan. 'I've got the girl.'

'Good!' said the metallic voice at the other end of the private line. 'I'll come at once.'

Sullivan hung up the receiver and shut the cupboard. Lighting a cigarette he sat down on an empty packing case and waited.

He waited for quite a while and then he

heard the sound of a key grating in the lock of the outer door. The inner door opened and a man came in. He was dressed in a soiled raincoat and large, dark glasses covered his eyes. Round his throat he wore a scarf that was pulled up over the lower part of his face. A cloth cap was pulled down so that it nearly met the glasses. His face was completely concealed and his hands were covered with leather gloves.

He stood for a moment just inside the door, and then he came further into the room.

'Where is she?' he asked.

'Over there against the wall,' said Sullivan.

The newcomer took a torch from his pocket and moved over to the unconscious girl, propped up against the wall. Her head had fallen forward on her breast.

Mister Big pressed the button of the torch and focused the bright light on her head and shoulders, raising her head with his free hand.

Sullivan heard the hiss of his breath

and the oath that followed.

'What's the matter?' he began.

'Matter?' snarled the other furiously. 'Why, you blasted fool, you've got the wrong girl!'

11

'What's the matter, miss?'

The voice penetrated into Eileen Barnard's dazed brain and she stirred uneasily.

'Are you feeling ill, miss?' said the voice.

She opened her eyes. Her head ached violently and a cold wind blew in her face. She put up her hand to ward off the bright light that hurt her eyes, and discovered that she was sitting somewhere in the open air and that a man was bending over her shining a lantern in her face.

'Where — where am I?' she whispered hoarsely. 'What — what happened?'

'You're in Hyde Park,' said the constable. 'I'd like to know what you're doing here.'

He shifted the light from her eyes and she looked round, grateful for the cool darkness.

'How did you get here. What's the matter with you?' asked the man suspiciously. 'You haven't been drinking . . . '

'Of course, I haven't!' said Eileen indignantly.

'Well, what are you doing here?' he demanded.

'I don't know,' she declared truthfully. 'I don't remember what happened after I got into that taxi in Victoria Street.'

Her voice cracked and she shivered.

'Got in a taxi in Victoria Street, did you?' said the policeman. 'When was this?'

'About half past seven,' she began, and he interrupted with an exclamation.'

'It's after midnight now,' he said. The suspicion deepened in his voice. 'Where did you go in this taxi?'

'I didn't go anywhere, not that I know,' she replied. 'I was going to Victoria Station to get a train home. There was a man in the cab already. He stuck something into my arm and that's all I remember.'

The constable cleared his throat. He surveyed the pretty, fair-haired girl in the pink raincoat and shook his head dubiously.

'What's your name?' he asked.

Eileen gave her name and her address.

'You'd better come along with me to the station,' said the constable. 'This wants looking into . . . '

'If you'll get in touch with my friends,' said Eileen, 'they will be able to tell you that I left their flat in Wellington Mansions . . . '

'Wellington Mansions?' repeated the constable. 'That's where the murders was committed . . . '

Eileen started to nod her head but the movement brought such a stab of pain through her brain that she cried out.

'You come along with me, miss,' said the policeman. 'Can you walk?'

'I'll try,' she answered.

She struggled to her feet, but her knees gave way and she would have fallen if the constable had not supported her. She stood clinging to him, her head swimming. It was only the result of her first sudden movement. In a little while the dizziness passed off and she felt better.

How she got there she was never quite certain but at last she found herself in a warm room drinking hot coffee, and telling her story to an inspector who questioned her closely about her adventure of the night.

The drug was still in her system and soon she began to feel queer again. She must have lost consciousness for the next thing she knew she was in a narrow bed with a nurse bending over her and two men standing at the foot.

One was a stout man with sleepy-looking eyes; the other lean and ungainly with a shock of the reddest hair she had ever seen.

'She's had a long sleep,' said the nurse. 'I think she'll be all right. How do you feel, Miss Barnard?'

'I feel fine,' said Eileen. She certainly felt very much better. Her head was clear, and the light no longer hurt her eyes.

'This is an extraordinary experience of yours,' remarked Mr. Budd gently. 'I'm a police officer an' this is a friend of mine, Mr. Dugan. I'd like to know more about this adventure of yours.'

Eileen smiled.

'I can't tell you any more than I told the police last night,' she said. She repeated her story.

'I suppose,' remarked Mr. Budd, when she had finished, 'you haven't any idea where this place is you was taken too?'

'Not the faintest. I don't remember anything after the man in the taxi stuck the needle in my arm.'

'You weren't robbed?'

She shook her head.

'I hadn't anything worth taking. Only a pound note and some silver in my bag. That was beside me when I woke up on that seat in Hyde Park.'

'You picked up the taxi in Victoria Street?'

Again she nodded.

'I'd just left Wellington Mansions,' she explained. 'I'd been to the Stayners . . . ' She caught sight of the pink raincoat on a chair. 'Oh, that's Margaret's coat. I must let her have it back.'

'You were wearing Miss Stayner's raincoat?' It was the red-haired man who spoke and into his grey eyes shot a gleam of interest. 'Of course, you must be the friend who was supposed to have phoned her the other night?'

'That's right,' she said.

'I begin to see a gleam of light,' murmured Mr. Budd softly and his tired eyes opened very wide for a fraction of a minute. 'In fact the illumination is becomin' dazzlin'. You were mistaken for Margaret Stayner.'

Colin nodded.

'Seems fairly obvious,' he agreed.

Eileen looked from one to the other.

'Mistook me for Margaret? Why should anyone want to kidnap Margaret?'

'I'd like to know that,' said Mr. Budd. 'But it appears that they do. I think that the accident she had on the way was the luckiest thing that could have happened — for her!' He scratched his fat chin. 'I don't think she'd ever have reached you.'

'I was sure there was a lot behind that telephone message,' said Colin.

'But how does it link up with Mister Big?' grunted the stout superintendent. 'Oh, well. Never mind now. I think we should let Miss Barnard have a good rest.

Don't you go worryin' about anythin'. We got in touch with your home an' your father is on his way to take you back. I'm sorry we had to disturb you. I'd like to see you again later, but I won't disturb you any longer now.'

Colin said goodbye to the girl and they left the hospital together. Mr. Budd was going back to Scotland Yard, and Colin persuaded him, much against his will, to walk part of the way.

'Pretty girl, isn't she?' remarked the reporter.

'Who?' asked Mr. Budd absently.

'Eileen Barnard, of course.'

'I didn't notice,' said the superintendent.

Colin snorted.

'You're not human! She's the prettiest girl I've seen for a long time.'

'I didn't know you were a judge,' said Mr. Budd. They walked along for a while in silence. Then Colin said:

'I should put a man on to watch Margaret Stayner, if I were you.'

'Do 'ye know, I was just thinkin' the same,' remarked Mr. Budd.

'Great minds think alike,' grinned Colin. Mr. Budd sighed.

'You might've thought of somethin' more original,' he said. 'I'm not walkin' any further. I'm catchin' the next bus on the corner.'

He walked to the bus stop and waited for a bus that would set him down in Whitehall. A man hurrying along the pavement bumped into him, apologised, and hurried on. The stout superintendent thought nothing of the incident at the time. Later he was to remember it.

His bus came along and he climbed inside. During the short journey he thought about the case he was engaged on. He had experienced a number of difficult cases before but this was really a snorter!

There was nothing tangible to get hold of. Mister Big remained a myth, but a myth who gave tangible evidence of his existence. The murder of Jameson and the taxi-driver were only incidents. And that was the difficulty. There was no sign of any coherent plan. Nothing but a series of apparently isolated incidents that seemed to have no connection.

He had not got very far with his thinking when he reached his destination, got off the bus, and entered the Yard by the Whitehall entrance.

There were a number of reports waiting on his desk and he settled down to read and initial them. This took him nearly two hours. When he had finished he leaned back in his chair with a sigh of relief. He hated paper work which took up too much valuable time and was getting worse. The country was getting swamped with bureaucrats and civil servants, he reflected. People who could've been engaged in productive effort instead of drawing salaries for doing very little. That was getting worse too. More nationalisation meant more of these drones. Look at the railways, they'd made a profit under private enterprise; provided a service that was certainly infinitely better than the present one. And that cost the country millions. Quite ridiculous! An Alice in Wonderland way to go about things. And it wasn't confined to the railways.

Mr. Budd took out one of his thin, black cigars. He sniffed it appreciatively.

Cutting off the end, he produced his lighter, and was in the act of pressing the spring when the thing slipped from his fingers.

The accident saved his life! As the lighter touched the floor there was a blinding flash and a shattering explosion! The desk was lifted and hurled against Mr. Budd, throwing him backwards on the floor!

Dazed, but otherwise unhurt, Mr. Budd picked himself up and examined the state of the damage. Of the lighter nothing was visible. Where the thing had fallen was a jagged hole in the floor. It was the desk which had saved him. If he had been holding the lighter . . .

Mr. Budd compressed his lips. He understood why the man had bumped against him at the bus stop. He had substituted the lighters. A clever 'dip' could have done it with ease. The lighter had been charged with a high explosive and detonated by pressing the spring. Mister Big had made his first attempt!

12

The sound of the explosion brought startled men to the wrecked office and they listened in consternation to Mr. Budd's explanation.

'Good God!' ejaculated a grey-haired inspector. 'You might have been killed!'

'I think that was the intention,' said Mr. Budd. 'I take a lot of killin'.' He looked round the office and shook his head. 'I shall have to find some temporary quarters while this is bein' repaired,' he said.

He was fixed up with a room further along the corridor whose occupant was away on leave. He moved in with his belongings and had barely done so when a note was brought to him. It was enclosed in a cheap envelope and he knew who it came from before he ripped it open and took out the contents.

He read the scrawled letter three times, and pursed his lips. He laid it down on his writing-table. He sat rubbing his chin thoughtfully for some time and then he pulled the telephone towards him and spoke to the switchboard.

'Get me the *Post-Bulletin*,' he said, and waited.

In a few seconds he was connected to that enterprising newspaper and, after some delay, succeeded in getting hold of Colin Dugan.

'I've just had a note from Gabby Smith,' he said. 'I don't suppose you know who that is but he's a little grass. He's often supplied us with information and is pretty reliable. He says he's found Mister Big's headquarters. Thought you might be interested.'

Colin was interested and said so.

'I'll come along at once,' he said.

'Do,' said the stout superintendent. 'I've somethin' else that'll interest you, too!'

He pushed the telephone away, and lit a cigar. But this time he used a match! His superiors would probably have had ideas about this collaboration with a newspaper man, but Mr. Budd had a great respect for Colin Dugan's intelligence. They had worked together before with good results. He was completely trustworthy: would print nothing without Mr. Budd's sanction and could be taken into the superintendent's confidence.

He arrived twenty minutes later and was surprised to find Mr. Budd had moved from his old office.

'Why the new digs?' he demanded flinging his hat on the chair.

Mr. Budd told him.

'Phew! That was a narrow escape,' exclaimed Colin. 'You could have been badly injured.'

'An' there would've been rejoicin' in the Big Man's camp. As it is there'll be a wailin' an' gnashin' of teeth.' Mr. Budd picked up the dirty note from in front of him and gave it to Colin. 'Look at this,' he said.

The reporter read the illiterate scrawl:

I ment to come and see you but beleve I am suspectted so I am riting this mister big has got a place in upperthames street an orfice in the name of jacob

were he meets a man caled sulivan e is
meeting him there ternite at 8.30 I will
be under the arch near lundun bridg
and show you the place S.

Colin's eyes gleamed as he finished
deciphering this epistle.

'If this is true we ought to get Mister
Big tonight,' he said.

'I hope so,' said Mr. Budd fervently. He
was a very tired man for he had had little
rest since the murders at Wellington
Mansions. 'I'm goin' to arrange for a
raid,' he went on. 'I thought you might
like to come along.'

'You bet I would,' asserted Colin.

'You'd better meet me here at seven-
thirty,' said the superintendent. 'I'll plan
the raid for eight-forty. That will give us
plenty of time.'

'Do you mind if I bring Trent?' asked
the reporter.

Mr. Budd hesitated.

'I suppose you can,' he said. 'Yes, bring
him along if you want to.'

When Dugan had gone he pressed a
button on his desk. To the constable who

presently answered the summons he said:

'Find Sergeant Leek and send him to me,' said Mr. Budd. After a little delay the lank form of the sergeant entered, and stood blinking, his melancholy face even more lugubrious than usual.

'We're makin' a raid on an office in Upper Thames Street to-night,' grunted Mr. Budd. 'I shall want twenty men. They had better come in a van of some kind. Arrange that, will you?'

The sergeant nodded.

'I'll attend to it,' he said. 'What time?'

'Be ready to leave here at seven-forty,' said Mr. Budd.

'D'you think anythin' 'ull come of it?' asked Leek gloomily.

'It's the best chance we've had to date,' replied the stout superintendent. For half an hour he discussed the arrangements with the sergeant. When he had finished Leek went over to the door.

'I'll be seein' you later,' he said.

'Don't be late,' warned Mr. Budd. 'If you sleep all the afternoon you may wake up feelin' that the world is a better an' brighter place.'

Sergeant Leek went slowly down the corridor, a frown on his long face. Calling in at the canteen he had a cup of tea and presently left the building by the White-hall entrance. He was quite unconscious of the inconspicuous man who followed him as he walked in the direction of Charing Cross.

Reaching Soho, he entered a coffee bar in Greek Street. A man sitting at one of the tables reading a newspaper looked up and nodded as Leek went over to the counter and bought a cup of coffee. He carried the cup over to the table where the man with the paper was sitting.

'Well?' The man looked at him questioningly. 'What have you got to tell me?'

Leek sat down.

'There's goin' to be a raid tonight, eight-thirty,' he said under his breath. 'We're takin' twenty men and surroundin' the place.'

His companion grunted.

'Tell me all about it,' he said.

The sergeant proceeded to talk rapidly but in so low a tone that the other had to lean forward to catch what he said. When he had finished the man laid his folded paper on the table and got up.

'I'm off,' he said. 'Keep in touch with me and let me know if you get hold of anything else.'

With a curt nod he went out and a few minutes later the melancholy sergeant followed him, taking the newspaper the man had left.

Reaching his lodgings and locking the door of his room, he took a thin packet of notes from the folds of the newspaper, put it away in a drawer, and lying down on his bed was soon fast asleep.

* * *

Upper Thames Street was deserted; a dreary waste with refuse-strewn gutters and pavements that glistened in the meagre light of the street's standards.

It had started to rain, a thin drizzle that promised to continue all night. Except for the rats no sign of life stirred. The rats scurried from one side of the street to the other, nosing among the refuse in the gutters; fat, sleek shapes, with vicious teeth, that squeaked angrily when one of their own tribe deprived another of a dainty morsel.

Presently, during the night, an army of these rodents would come up from the river and cross to the warehouses in search of food. Hundreds of them, dangerous if cornered, swarming in this infested district, over-running the offices as well, leaving the marks of their filthy feet on walls and woodwork.

Eight o'clock was striking when a large covered lorry came slowly down the street, and backed into the space before a wide gate leading on to a wharf. The vague forms of men slipped out of the lorry and took up positions in dark doorways and passages.

The whole of this unusual activity was over in a matter of minutes and then the street was deserted again. This time even more so, for the rats had vanished, hiding, like the men who had come out of the lorry behind anything that offered cover.

Curiously enough this was only applicable to the immediate vicinity of the building that housed the offices of the mysterious Mr. Jacobs.

At the expiration of a quarter of an hour, a man came walking swiftly from the direction of London Bridge. He wore a dirty raincoat and a cap that was pulled low over his eyes. It was difficult to see what he looked like. Without pausing, he turned into the entrance to Mr. Jacobs' building.

Mr. Budd, watching in company with Gordon Trent and Colin Dugan from the convenient concealment of a narrow alley almost opposite, pressed Colin's arm.

'Number one,' he whispered, and turned to the thin, wizen-faced little shrimp of a man who stood shivering at his side. 'How many are comin' to this party?'

Gabby Smith shook his head.

'Dunno,' he whined in a strong cockney twang. 'I on'y know about Sullivan. I don't know nuthin' about no others.'

'How does Mister Big come?' asked Colin.

Smith shook his head again.

'I dunno 'ow 'e comes,' he answered.

There were beads of perspiration on the little man's face and he was shaking with either excitement or fear. It was a curious fact, which the stout superintendent had noticed before, that not once did he refer to Mister Big as anything else than 'he.'

'Is there another entrance at the back?' asked Mr. Budd.

'No, there ain't.'

'Then how the devil *does* he get in?' demanded Mr. Budd irritably.

'Couldn't tell yer. Nobody ain't ever seed 'im go in or come out.'

'He can't live there,' grunted the superintendent, 'so there must be some other way in. Well, he won't get away this time. Once he's inside we've got him bottled up. The place is surrounded. He'll have to perform a miracle to get through my cordon without being spotted.'

He broke off. Another man had appeared at the other end of the street. He was short, rather stocky, and walked with an assured swing to his broad shoulders.

'That's Al Davis,' said Gabby in his nasal whine.

This man too disappeared into the gloomy entrance to the building housing Mr. Jacobs.

'Give it another ten minutes an' then we can start the fireworks,' grunted Mr. Budd.

'You won't want me any more, will yer?' whined the little man pleadingly.

'All right, you can hop it,' said Mr. Budd, and with a scared look round him, Gabby Smith shuffled off rapidly, keeping in the shadows until he vanished from sight.

The other three waited patiently after he had gone, until a single stroke from the church clock denoted the half hour.

Mr. Budd waited five minutes and then he stepped from the darkness of the alley, took a torch from his pocket and flashed it twice.

Instantly three other men materialised from the surrounding gloom and joined him. They had a muttered exchange and then all six crossed the road and entered the doorway of Mr. Jacobs' building.

'We shall have to break down the door with as little noise as possible,' whispered

Mr. Budd as they prepared to ascend the narrow stairs. 'It'll give 'em a few seconds warning, but we can't help that.'

Followed by Colin and Gordon, he led the way, flashing his torch to light the steps, and quietly they mounted to the third floor. Mr. Jacobs' door was shut.

They stopped outside it. Mr. Budd drew a revolver from his pocket.

'Now,' he murmured softly.

The two burliest of the men with him hurled themselves against the door. It cracked but the lock held.

'Again!' rapped Mr. Budd.

At the second onslaught the door crashed open with a splintering of wood.

Mr. Budd was the first to cross the threshold, and as he did so there came a startled cry of alarm from an open doorway facing him.

And then the dim light in the outer office went out.

'Guard the door,' ordered Mr. Budd, and lumbering over to the flap in the counter flung it back. Almost as the words left his lips, a vicious pencil of flame split the darkness and a bullet snarled past the superintendent's head.

Two more shots followed so closely together that they almost sounded as one. One of the men who had entered behind him, gave a cry and collapsed on the floor clasping his leg.

Mr. Budd dropped to cover behind the counter.

'Blow your whistle!' he shouted. The whistle was drowned in the fusillade of shots which whined round him. A muffled laugh came from somewhere, and then a rush of feet on the stairs, and a dozen men poured into the room.

'The people we want are in there,' said Mr. Budd, and led the way to the door of the inner office. The door fell with a crash and they saw the stocky man, Davis, cramming a fresh clip of cartridges into his automatic.

Colin knocked the weapon out of his hand and the man, with a snarl of rage, closed with him. They both fell to the floor fighting desperately. Davis was enormously strong and got his hands round Colin's throat. Gordon saw what was happening and went to his friend's assistance. Gripping the man round the neck he half strangled him until he was forced to let go.

Davis writhed and twisted to try and free himself. He might have succeeded if Colin hadn't jumped up and banged his head on the floor, after which he took no further interest in the proceedings.

Both panting heavily, Colin and Gordon looked about to see what was happening. In the light of the torches carried by the police they saw that Sullivan had been secured in handcuffs and stood sullenly staring at the floor.

'Where's the other man?' demanded Mr. Budd sharply.

'These two were the only ones in the building, sir,' answered one of his men. He indicated Sullivan and Davis.

'Are you sure nobody got away?'

'Nobody got past us,' answered the man guarding the door. 'Did they, Bill?'

The other man shook his head.

Mr. Budd went over to Sullivan.

'What's happened to the man called Mister Big?' he demanded.

'Find out!' Sullivan snarled the reply

through his teeth.

'Make a thorough search,' ordered the stout superintendent, 'and see if you can find another exit to this place.'

'Right, sir!'

Six of the men who had taken part in the raid left the room.

'You look after that feller who's wounded, will you?' went on Mr. Budd looking at Gordon and he nodded.

Colin Dugan was carefully testing the walls of the inner room to the sneering amusement of Sullivan.

'Looking for secret panels?' he scoffed. 'Been reading sensational thrillers, eh?'

'You won't be readin' 'em, you'll be livin' 'em,' snapped Mr. Budd. 'You'll go down for twenty years.'

'You've got nothing on me,' retorted Sullivan.

'Wait till you hear the charge,' answered Mr. Budd. 'It'll make you feel that Jack the Ripper was a boy scout!'

He turned his back on the scowling Sullivan and joined Colin.

'Found anythin'?'

Colin shook his head.

'Not yet. These walls are solid.'

Mr. Budd rubbed irritably at his bristly hair.

'He can't have vanished into thin air,' he grunted. 'There must be some way out.'

'Perhaps he wasn't here at all,' suggested Colin. 'If there was a back exit the men surrounding the building would've seen him.'

One of the men forming the search party came back at that moment.

'We've searched the entire building, sir,' he reported. 'There's no other way out or in.'

'That's that!' growled the disappointed superintendent. 'He can't have been here after all ... ' He broke off as Colin uttered an exclamation. 'What is it?'

'This part of the wall sounds hollow,' said the reporter and tapped a portion of the wall above a small table.

Mr. Budd tested it himself.

'You're right,' he declared. 'Let's see if there's anythin' behind it.'

Two of his men attacked the wall with clasp knives. A panel slid back revealing a screen of fine wire gauze. Into the small chamber beyond, Mr. Budd flashed a light and started back.

'Quick!' he cried exultantly. 'He's in there!'

Ripping the wire screen down he covered the figure crouching in the chair with his automatic.

'I want you!' he said. 'Put your hands up and come out.'

The man in the chair remained motionless. With sudden uneasiness Mr. Budd reached out and caught the man by the shoulder. The head fell on one side and the reason for his stillness was revealed.

The thing in the chair was a wax dummy!

13

A complete examination of the building revealed the ingenious method by which Mister Big had avoided the possibility of any of the people he employed betraying him.

He had never actually entered the office occupied by the mysterious Mr. Jacobs at all. The doors, the panel, and the lights were all electrically controlled from another office in a warehouse farther down the street.

They were able to trace this by the wires that ran down the side of the building to the warehouse. Behind the dummy they found a loudspeaker and a microphone leading to a second loudspeaker and microphone in the warehouse office. By this means he had been able to talk to the people who came to him and hear their replies as easily as if he had really been seated behind the wire gauze as they supposed.

He was completely immune from capture. His safety was assured.

'Quite a clever idea,' remarked Mr. Budd. 'This feller's got brains whoever he is.'

It was long after midnight by the time they had finished, and, tired out, Gordon fell into bed and was almost instantly asleep. He was still in bed when Colin called on the following morning. Getting up he pulled on a dressing-gown, and went into the sitting-room.

'Well, how are you feeling this morning?' greeted Colin.

'I shall be better when I've had some breakfast,' grunted Gordon. 'I'm famished.'

'I had mine hours ago,' said the other virtuously. 'But don't let me stop you. Eat, drink and be merry . . .'

'Don't complete the quotation,' said Gordon. 'Help yourself to cigarettes. I'll bring you some tea when it's made.'

He went out into the kitchen and put the kettle on, laid a tray, and rummaged in the fridge for bacon and eggs. When the tea was made and the breakfast cooked he carried it in to the sitting-room.

'You're an early bird,' he said as he poured out tea and handed a cup to Colin. 'Guilty conscience?'

'I'm on my way to see Budd,' replied Colin. 'I came here first because I thought you might like to come with me.'

'What's on?' mumbled Gordon, his mouth full of egg and bacon. 'I shall never get any work done until they get this chap Mister Big . . . '

'Don't come if you're busy . . . '

'Of course, I'm coming. I won't be long.' He hastily finished his breakfast, had a quick bath and shave, shoved the dirty dishes in the sink, and announced himself ready.

Mr. Budd looked a very weary man when they were shown into his office.

'I've been workin' most of the night with precious little to show for it,' he growled. 'This feller's clever. That conjurin' trick he worked in Upper Thames Street was pretty smart.'

'How did he know when anybody called?' asked Gordon.

'They gave a special signal on a buzzer which rang in his private bolt-hole in the warehouse,' replied Mr. Budd. 'I got that bit out of Sullivan with a lot of persuasion. When he got the signal he operated the control for the door and the lights. Simple, isn't it?'

'Can't you trace him by the people who rented him the office?' asked Colin.

'You'd think so, wouldn't you? But we can't. The buildin's owned by the firm that occupies the ground floor. They're fishmongers on a large scale. Two years ago they let this one room to a feller who called himself an inventor. He was a thin chap with dark hair and a little black moustache — looked like a foreigner, according to them. Said his name was Lubeck. He paid a year's rent in lieu of the usual references, said he didn't know anyone in London and paid in cash. He brought a lot of electrical and mechanical stuff. Of course, nobody questioned this because he said he was an inventor. In fact, they didn't take much notice of him at all.'

'Pity!'

Colin Dugan frowned.

'What about the other place — Jacobs' office? Who took that?' he said.

'I drew another blank there,' sighed Mr. Budd. 'It was rented about the same time by a little Jewish chap who said he was in the canned goods trade. Like the other feller, Lubeck, he paid in advance. I got a description of Jacobs. There are about a hundred thousand people walking about the streets of London exactly like him!'

Colin lit a cigarette, blew out a cloud of smoke and watched it drift towards the ceiling.

'So the raid didn't help very much?' he said.

'Oh, I don't know. We've got Sullivan an' Davis. Sullivan was a sort of chief-of-staff, I think,' said Mr. Budd.

'Sullivan ought to know the identity of Mister Big?' put in Gordon.

Mr. Budd shook his head.

'He doesn't. He's never seen him!' he answered gloomily. 'There are two things that I haven't told you yet. We found a concealed telephone in the warehouse room. It was a private line . . . '

'I say, that's something, surely?' interrupted Colin excitedly. 'Where to?'

'To a room in another warehouse,' growled Mr. Budd. 'This feller seems to have got rooms in half the street. It's only a ramshackle place an' it's empty! I'm goin' along there in a minute. You can come along, if you like.'

'You bet we will,' said Colin. 'What was the other thing?'

'The identity of the feller who attacked Stayner,' said the stout superintendent.

'Who was it?' asked Gordon.

'A man named William Sutton. He left his dabs on the handle of that knife an' C.R.O. traced 'em. Twenty years ago he was tried for the murder of a man named Paget. The jury disagreed. There was no doubt about his guilt but they thought there were extenuatin' circumstances. Instead of bein' hanged he was sentenced to twenty years. He was released five days ago.'

'Why should he want to stab Stayner?' demanded Gordon.

'You can search me!' said Mr. Budd.

'Unless he was actin' for Mister Big. Somebody could've met him from prison an' offered him the job. If the money was good he'd probably have jumped at it.'

He got up laboriously.

'We'll get along to this warehouse,' he said. 'I must get back here by twelve to attend a conference.'

A police car took them to Upper Thames Street and set them down at the narrow passage along which Sullivan had carried Eileen Barnard. A constable was on guard at the door to the warehouse and saluted Mr. Budd as they entered.

Colin and Gordon stared round the bare room rather disappointedly.

'Nothing much here, is there?' said the reporter after Mr. Budd had shown him the telephone. 'Is the rest of the place the same?'

'Practically. I hadn't time for more than a quick glance round. That's why I've come now.'

They went over the whole building but found nothing to reward their diligence. The upper floors were as bare as the lower.

It was not until they had returned to the ground floor, and Colin was searching among a pile of broken packing-cases that they made any fresh discovery at all. And then, moving a crate full of rotting straw, he saw the outline of a trap-door in the floor.

His exclamation brought Mr. Budd and Gordon over to his side.

'There's a cellar or something under here,' cried the reporter. 'Help me move this rubbish.'

They pulled the pile of old packing-cases and crates away from the corner and revealed an oblong trap with a rusty iron ring.

'This has recently been used,' grunted Mr. Budd breathlessly. 'There's no dust where the ring rests.'

He grasped the ring and pulled. The trap came up easily and without noise. When it was fully open they saw that the hinges were thick with grease.

A flight of wooden steps led down-wards into darkness, but the air that came up to them was fresh and clean-smelling. Mr. Budd pulled out a torch and directed the light down into the darkness. They saw that the wooden steps ended on a stone floor. Leaning over the edge of the trap he was able to make out a large cellar-like room with walls of brick.

Getting up he began to descend the steps with Colin and Gordon behind him. They found themselves in a huge low-ceilinged room that was almost the same size as the ground floor of the warehouse above. Beneath their feet was concrete and the roof was formed of the beams that supported the floor of the room over-head.

Along one wall ran a bench, obviously recently put in because the woodwork was new, and on this were a collection of glass vessels, flasks, retorts, test-tubes, condensers, all the paraphernalia of the chemist.

'Why the place is a laboratory!' exclaimed Gordon. 'Look at all those bottles on that shelf above the bench.'

'And a bedroom too, by the look of that,' said Colin, pointing to the narrow camp bed in one corner.

Mr. Budd's eyes narrowed as he saw it.

Without comment, he went over and stood looking down at the heap of untidy blankets that lay on the hard mattress.

'Somebody's been livin' here,' he grunted.

'You don't require much imagination to guess who,' said Colin. 'See that?'

He nodded in the direction of a long steel chain attached to a staple in the wall, on one end of which was circle of steel like a large handcuff.

'This is the place where Jameson was kept prisoner,' he continued. He bent down and examined the manacle. It had been eaten away in one place by some strong acid. 'If you think it's just a coincidence that this place is fitted as a laboratory remember that Jameson was a chemist.'

'What was the object of keeping him here?' asked Gordon.

'I should say it had something to do with those experiments he was carrying out in West Germany,' said Colin. 'Let's see if the apparatus will help us. I used to know a smattering of chemistry.'

He went over and searched among the glass vessels on the bench, and peered at the rows of bottles on the shelf. Finally he shook his head.

'I can't tell much from this,' he admitted. 'There is nothing to show what he was working at.'

'There's some drawers here,' said Mr. Budd, stooping down. 'Perhaps there's somethin' in them that'll help.'

He pulled one out. It was long and shallow and contained only a number of small black notebooks, filled with figures and chemical formulae.

'These don't mean a thing to me,' he declared after a quick glance through them, 'but I expect our experts at the Yard'll be able to tell us what they're all about.'

He put them down on the bench and opened the other two drawers. One was full of glass rods, filter papers, spatulas, platinum wire and various odds and ends. The other contained a shallow wooden box and nothing else.

Mr. Budd raised the lid. It was full of a white powder that glistened in the light.

'Looks like salt,' he said.

'Just a minute,' said Colin. He thrust a

bony finger into the powder and cautiously applied it to his tongue. 'That's cocaine!' he announced and wiped his mouth with his handkerchief. 'There's enough to . . . '

A loud thud drowned the rest of his words. The trap had shut with a bang. Mr. Budd turned his torch towards the steps as Gordon ran over and hurried up to the trap. He pressed with all his strength against it but it was immovable!

Somebody had shut it and fastened it! They were prisoners!

14

Colin joined Gordon on the steps and together they thrust at the closed trap. But it would not budge an inch.

'Who the deuce shut it?' demanded Mr. Budd. 'It couldn't have been the constable . . . '

'Somebody's not only shut it but fastened it,' panted Gordon. 'It won't shift.'

'Let's bang on it,' suggested Colin. 'Perhaps the constable will hear.'

They tried. They banged on the wooden trap and shouted but there was no sound from above. At last, tired and hoarse, they stopped for a rest.

'It looks as if we're going to be cooped up here for some time, unless we can make that constable hear,' said Colin.

'Surely we made enough row to attract his attention,' grunted Mr. Budd.

'It looks suspicious to me,' said Colin seriously.

Gordon looked at him quickly.

'You don't think . . . ?' he began.

'That trap didn't shut and fasten itself,' broke in the reporter. 'I think someone has deliberately trapped us.'

'But the constable . . . How did they get past him?' demanded Gordon.

Colin shrugged his shoulders.

'Maybe they didn't!' he replied significantly.

'Well, whatever happened,' put in Mr. Budd, 'we'd better try an' find a way out of here.'

He began to make a close inspection of the cellar in the hope of finding some other way out but he was disappointed. There was a small ventilator but it was only eight inches square.

While he was thus engaged, Colin and Gordon had tried another onslaught on the trap but the wood was thick and solid and withstood all their efforts.

'No good!' grunted Colin. 'The thing's made of solid oak. We'd need a battering ram to get through it.'

He stopped suddenly and sniffed.

'Can you smell anything?' he asked.

142

Mr. Budd raised his head in alarm. An acrid, burning smell reached his nostrils. It was faint but unmistakable. The smell of smoke!

'Listen!' he said.

They listened with straining ears and they heard the faint sound of crackling.

'It's fire!' cried Colin. 'The warehouse above!'

The smell was stronger and a thin wisp of smoke filtered past the trap.

Gordon ran up the steps and put his hand on the wood.

'It's hot!' he exclaimed.

'I can hear the fire clearly,' said Mr. Budd. 'It must be a pretty big one by the sound.'

They listened. Added to the previous faint crackling was a roar, angry and menacing.

'We'll be roasted like hedgehogs in a camp fire unless we can get out!' cried Colin. 'The only way, apparently, is through the trap.'

'But how can we break it open?'

Gordon looked round as he spoke and then hurried over to the camp bed. He

143

pulled off the blankets and threw them on the floor. The bed was made of iron and he pulled and wrenched to get hold of something with which to attack the trap.

Mr. Budd and Colin helped him and presently they managed between them to get hold of two stout pieces of iron that had formed the sides of the bed-frame.

Carrying these over to the steps they tried to insert them between the edges of the trap and the floor above. But it fitted too closely.

At the end of twenty minutes they were forced to stop. The atmosphere was getting unpleasantly hot and a faint, bluish haze hung in the air. The roar of the fire had increased. It would not be long before the floor above, which formed the ceiling of the cellar, was ablaze.

The heat was getting stifling and the blue haze was rapidly increasing to a grey cloud that set them coughing.

'I'm going to have another go at that trap,' said Colin.

'You're wasting your time,' said Gordon. 'Nothing but dynamite would shift that . . .'

Colin swung round.

'Dynamite!' he cried, and there was sudden hope in his voice. 'Quick! Bring the torch over here!'

He ran over to the bench. Mr. Budd and Gordon followed him.

'There isn't any dynamite here,' grunted the stout superintendent.

'No.' Colin was peering along the row of stoppered bottles on the shelf above the bench. 'But we might be able to make a substitute. It won't be a very good one but it might do the trick.'

He took down three bottles.

'Did you ever make gun-powder when you were a boy?' he asked as he pulled over a large bowl and a measure.

'That's an idea!' said Gordon. 'Will it work?'

'I don't know,' said Colin. 'It won't be very powerful, but we'll hope for the best.'

He measured out the contents of the three bottles and began to mix them together in the bowl.

'This must be mixed as thoroughly as possible,' Colin went on. 'While I'm doing it see if you can loosen a brick in that wall.' He pointed to the wall facing

145

the bench. 'As far as I can calculate, it should be the outside wall of the warehouse.'

'Why not try an' blow the trap open?' said Mr. Budd.

'It wouldn't do any good,' said Colin. 'There's a raging furnace above. We should be cinders before we could get through.'

He went on with his mixing while Gordon and the stout superintendent set to work to try and loosen the brick, attacking the mortar round it with a pocket-knife.

It took them fifteen minutes to loosen it sufficiently to be able to lever it out and by the time they had done so, Colin was ready with a bowl full of black powder.

In one corner of the ceiling the fire had already broken through and long tongues of flame were licking the heavy beams.

'Let's pray that this will work,' muttered Colin.

He carried the bowl of powder over and began to press scoopfuls of powder into the hole left by the removal of the brick. He rammed it in tightly with the wooden end of a pestle from the bench. He had made a rough fuse of rolled up paper filled with part of the powder, and he inserted this well into the powder in the cavity. With strips torn from the blanket he wedged up the hole as tightly as possible round the projecting fuse.

'There we are!' he said. 'It may not work. We haven't been able to mix the ingredients as well as they would be in a proper powder-mill and that'll make a difference in the power. But we'll hope for the best!'

He took out his lighter.

'Better get over there,' he said.

They went over to the far corner and Colin snapped on the lighter and lit the fuse. It fizzed like a squib, and Colin ran over and joined the other two.

The fuse burned quickly with a shower of sparks and then . . .

The explosion was not very loud or very powerful but it was an explosion. The ignition of the powder in the confined space of the brick had been sufficient to loosen the other bricks, as they found when they coughed their way through the pungent fumes that filled the cellar.

With the iron parts of the bed, they attacked the wall and the loosened bricks fell, leaving a ragged gap through which cool, fresh air poured as they scrambled their way to safety.

15

The warehouse was blazing from ground floor to roof when they succeeded in making their way round from the crazy wharf on which they had emerged from the hole in the wall to Upper Thames Street.

Fire-engines blocked the narrow thoroughfare and although jets of water were pouring on the holocaust from a dozen different points it was obvious that the old building was doomed.

Mr. Budd found an inspector of the City Police, who listened in astonishment to what the superintendent had to tell him.

'I thought there was something fishy about the fire,' he said when Mr. Budd had finished. 'We found the constable in the alley-way with a broken head. Somebody had hit him pretty hard and the doctor says it'll be some time before he's able to talk, if he ever does. By then the building was alight in more than a dozen places. You had a narrow escape.'

'You can say that again!' growled Mr. Budd. 'If ever I get my hands on this feller, Mister Big as they call him, I'll make it as warm for him, I can promise you.'

He turned to Colin and Gordon.

'What we need is a good wash an' somethin' to eat,' he said. 'What are you lookin' at?'

The reporter was staring at the crowd watching the fire.

'I was wondering if Mister Big was among that bunch,' answered Colin.

'I shouldn't be surprised,' snarled Mr. Budd. 'But we shouldn't know him, even if he was standin' next to us. Come on, let's go!'

They moved away, forcing through the crowd. Somebody tapped Mr. Budd on the shoulder as they emerged on the outskirts, and he turned quickly. It was one of the men who had taken part in the raid on Mr. Jacobs' office.

'I was just going back to the Yard, sir, when I spotted you among the crowd,' said the man.

'Any news?' asked Mr. Budd.

'I was making a second search of Lubeck's office when I found this, sir.' He took a scrap of paper from a bulky pocket-book. 'We missed it the first time. It was wedged in the back of a drawer.'

Mr. Budd took the torn scrap of paper and read the three words on it:

William Sutton released . . .

The rest had been torn away.

'That ties up Sutton with the Big Man,' he commented. 'H'm! But how I don't know.'

He put the scrap of paper carefully away.

'I don't mind admittin' that I don't understand it,' he continued, frowning. 'Apart from the murder of Jameson an' the taxi-driver, there's this attempt to kidnap Miss Stayner. Now here's a man who comes out of prison and tries to stick a knife in her father. Mister Big killed Jameson an' the taxi-driver, he tried to abduct the girl, but why does this chap, Sutton, try to knife her father?'

'I think Sutton must have been employed by Mister Big,' said Gordon. 'You suggested that yourself.'

'Why should Mister Big want Stayner killed?' asked the superintendent. 'Did you find anythin' else?'

The police officer shook his head.

'No, sir. The office had been pretty thoroughly cleared out. There wasn't anything else.'

'We must be grateful for small mercies,' grunted Mr. Budd. 'I must go an' make myself presentable for that conference. I'd nearly forgotten all about it.'

He left Colin and Gordon and drove back to the Yard in the police car which had brought them and which was still waiting further up the street.

The conference was not a success. Colonel Blair was an outspoken man, and on the subject of Mister Big he spoke very plainly indeed.

Mr. Budd returned to his office rather ruffled and subsequent events did nothing to improve his temper.

He had barely settled himself behind his desk, and was contemplating the soothing influence of one of his thin black cigars, when a messenger entered with a note.

Mr. Budd ripped open the envelope and glanced at the contents. They were brief and to the point:

Pity you managed to escape. Next time you won't. Keep out of my business while you're alive — dead you will have no option.

There was no signature but there was no need for one.

Mr. Budd flung the note down on his desk and picked up the house phone.

'Get me the man on the door,' he snapped to the switch-board, and when he was connected: 'Who brought that note for me just now?'

The note had been delivered by a youth of about eighteen. He was wearing the usual leather jacket and jeans. Nothing to distinguish him from hundreds of others.

Mr. Budd slammed down the telephone and lighted his cigar. He was too cross to go out and eat. He sat glowering at his blotting-pad. There was very little to cheer him up. Colonel Blair's remarks had been very pungent indeed.

There was just one hope and the thought of it cleared a little of the gloom from his face. The idea that had come to him after the murders at Wellington Mansions, was well under way and might at any moment produce something.

When he had finished his cigar he left the Yard and went round to the little tea-shop nearby, where he ordered his usual meal of tea and hot buttered toast.

For an hour he sat munching and drinking and thinking, and when he returned to his office he felt better. At four o'clock that afternoon a report came through that the Thames Division had taken the body of a man out of the river near the Pool. He had not been drowned. He had been shot squarely between the eyes. The description of the dead man left no room for doubt as to who he was.

Mr. Budd went down to the station where the body had been taken. As he had expected it was the body of Gabby Smith.

'There was nothing on the body at all, sir,' said the station sergeant.

'I didn't expect there would be,' said Mr. Budd.

'He was a grass wasn't he?' asked the sergeant.

Mr. Budd nodded.

'Do you know if he had any relatives?'

'I don't know anythin' about him at all,' said the stout superintendent. 'I don't even know where he lived. Poor little devil! What a life, eh?'

'And what a death!' said the sergeant.

'He knew the risk he took,' said Mr. Budd. 'He preferred doin' what he did to an honest day's work. Queer! He'd have been better paid doin' some kind o' work.'

'And he'd still be alive,' said the sergeant.

And that was Gabby Smith's epitaph!

When Mr. Budd got back to the Yard there was an item of news awaiting him. The man who had been making inquiries concerning the original owner of the warehouse had made a discovery.

'It was owned by a man named William

155

Sutton, sir,' said the man standing beside the superintendent's desk.

'William Sutton, eh?' remarked Mr. Budd softly. 'Very interestin'. I'd like to meet this man Sutton. I think he might be able to tell us quite a lot.'

'Maybe they'll pull him in, sir,' said the man.

'Let's hope they will,' agreed Mr. Budd.

When he was alone again, he sent for Leek, but that lugubrious man was not to be found. He had left no message to say where he had gone or when he would be back.

Mr. Budd grunted.

'Gettin' independent in his old age,' he muttered. 'You just watch your step, Leek. Just watch your step!'

He sat on, his eyes closed and his hands clasped across his capacious stomach until he decided that he'd had enough for one day and prepared to go home.

He left the Yard by the Embankment entrance and as he turned out of the gates his hat was sent flying from his head. The

156

second bullet fanned his cheek; the third ripped a strip of cloth from his coat.

He jumped for the cover of a convenient pillar and glared at the stream of traffic that was passing. The shots might have come from any one of the numerous cars and trade vans. There had been no sound but a silencer would have accounted for that.

After a pause, Mr. Budd picked up his hat. A neat hole had been drilled through the crown. Death had passed very close indeed!

At that moment, seated in the interior of a harmless-looking laundry van, Sergeant Leek slipped a revolver into his pocket and issued fresh instructions to the driver.

His voice was despondent and he looked mournfully out through the front window at the passing traffic.

He was full of chagrin for he had missed his man!

16

Colin Dugan was given to boasting that except from the angle of news value women held no interest for him at all. He was rather contemptuous of the softer emotions, and during his few hours of leisure definitely preferred the company of his fellow men.

'I'm bachelor-minded,' he asserted when anyone raised the subject. 'Girls don't mean a thing in my life!'

Considering this point of view it is rather curious that immediately after his first meeting with Eileen Barnard he should have cast round in his mind for some excuse to see her again.

His connection with the *Post-Bulletin* provided one and he set off for the girl's house ostensibly on behalf of that enterprising journal.

Apparently the *Post-Bulletin* had developed a passionate interest in Miss Barnard, for the first visit resulted in a second and a third. On this last occasion it was apparently necessary to take Eileen out to dinner and a theatre. Their conversation during the evening would most certainly not have interested the readers of the *Post-Bulletin,* even if it had ever been printed. Which of course, it was not!

Gordon Trent came to hear of this sudden change in Colin's habits from Margaret, and when next he saw his friend, he mentioned the matter.

Colin's face assumed a hue that nearly matched his hair.

'Purely business,' he declared. 'Got to work some human interest into this Mister Big stuff.'

'That was all, was it?' asked Trent.

'Oh, well, of course, she's a very nice girl, you know. Got quite a good line of talk for a woman. I thought she might prove helpful . . . '

'There's no need to make excuses,' interrupted Gordon. 'It happens to the best of us sooner or later.'

Colin smiled — it was a rather sickly, sheepish smile. Hastily he changed the subject.

'Things seem rather at a standstill,' he said. 'I saw Budd this morning. He seemed rather gloomy. The Big Man has suddenly dried up altogether.'

Five days had elapsed since Mr. Budd had been shot at on the Embankment. In truth nothing fresh had happened. The stout superintendent had searched in vain for something to give him a lead. The fire had destroyed any traces there might have been at the warehouse, and Sullivan and Davis, so far as useful information was concerned, were no good at all. They both adopted an attitude of hostile and obstinate silence.

'They may know somethin' or they may not,' said Mr. Budd, talking the matter over with one of the chief constables at the Yard. 'If they do know anythin' we'll never get it out of 'em. A bit of the American third degree stuff might do it, but our methods won't.'

The grey-haired man was scandalised.

'We can't do anything like that,' he said, and Mr. Budd nodded despondently.

'I know we can't, sir,' he agreed. 'We've

got to treat 'em with kid gloves an' cotton-wool. They just laugh at us! It doesn't matter, of course, that several people have been killed. They're only the victims of violence. Nobody's interested in them! No half-baked psychologist is goin' to rant an' rave over them! It's only the murderers an' the thugs an' the hooligans that have to be looked after an' cosseted an' found excuses for! We mustn't do anythin' that might hurt *their* tender feelin's!'

He walked away, leaving the chief constable staring after him with dropped jaw and popping eyes.

Mr. Budd's usually equitable temper was becoming ruffled. His failure to make any headway over Mister Big was getting on his nerves.

The murder of Gabby Smith had been given prominence in the newspapers. Mr. Budd's favourite evening paper had, on the previous evening, carried a leading article concerning the incompetence of the police. It had leaked out that Smith had been a police informer and the editor had seized on this with avidity.

The police cannot even protect the lives of those who work for them (stated the *Evening Planet*). *This man Gabby Smith is known to have supplied them on various occasions with useful information. His work was highly dangerous and he should have been given adequate protection. Is it likely after the fate of this man that anyone possessing knowledge that could help the police will come forward?*

There was a great deal more on the same lines, and the article ended by demanding that the methods of the police be reviewed and considerably tightened up.

The stout superintendent had thrown the paper away, but the contents of the article had remained in his mind and rankled. To a certain extent he did feel responsible for Gabby's death. It was true that Smith was well paid for the information he had managed to get hold of. It was also true that he knew the risks that attached to his calling — if such a degraded form of livelihood can be so catalogued. But despite this, Mr. Budd had felt a little remorseful when he had seen that pathetic figure lying in the mortuary at Thames police station.

Nothing more had been seen or heard of the man who had attacked Stayner. Despite the fact that he was being searched for all over the country, he had completely vanished.

Mr. Budd had questioned Stayner about him, but the M.P. had denied all knowledge of William Sutton. He had never heard of the man before, and could offer no suggestion as to why he should have attempted his life.

There was no reason to suppose that he was lying. It was just one more unexplained event. He felt that he was collecting a series of these events, rather like a theatregoer who had seen the first act of a play and come out for a smoke in the interval. He was waiting for the bell that would warn him the curtain was rising on the second act, and curiously enough it was a bell that did warn him.

He was in the habit of staying late at the Yard; sitting huddled up in his padded chair behind his desk and chewing thoughtfully on the end of one of his villainous black cigars. It was in these quiet moments that he worked out most of his ideas and sorted through the facts in his possession. But this evening he decided to leave early.

He was back in his own office which had been repaired since the explosion, and he was just considering going home when the telephone bell rang. Stretching out a stubby hand, Mr. Budd pulled the instrument towards him and lifted the receiver.

'There's a Mr. John Stayner on the line for you,' said the switch-board.

'Put him through,' said Mr. Budd.

The voice of the M.P. came over the wire.

'Is that Superintendent Budd?' it asked.

'Speakin',' grunted Mr. Budd. 'What is it?'

'I've just got back from the House,' said Stayner. 'If you've finished with my daughter I'll come and fetch her home.'

'Your daughter?' repeated Mr. Budd.

'Has she left?' asked Stayner.

Mr. Budd's jaw tightened. He nearly

bit through the cigar stub.

'She hasn't been here . . . ' he began, and Stayner broke in quickly.

'But you sent for her earlier this evening,' he said.

'No!' snapped Mr. Budd curtly.

The voice of the M.P. grew suddenly agitated.

'She left a note to say she was seeing you,' he said. 'It was urgent and you sent a cab . . . '

'I didn't send a cab and I haven't seen Miss Stayner,' cut in Mr. Budd sharply. 'I'll come over right away.'

He slammed down the receiver, pulled the house telephone towards him and ordered a police car to be waiting at once. Struggling into his overcoat he picked up his hat and hurried down the stairs. The car came round just as he came out of the entrance and a few moments later he was ringing the bell at the Stayners' flat in Wellington Mansions.

Stayner himself opened the door and almost dragged Mr. Budd into the sitting-room.

'This is dreadful,' he said huskily.

'What can have happened to Margaret? Where . . . ?'

'Wait a minute,' said Mr. Budd checking him. 'It won't help to rush things. Tell me exactly what happened?'

Stayner poured out a stiff Johnnie Walker and drank it at a gulp.

What he had to tell was not very helpful. He had been over at the House most of the day. He had returned home to find a message from his daughter saying that Superintendent Budd had sent for her to go to Scotland Yard. The daily woman who usually left at six had stayed at Margaret's request to get a meal ready for her father. It was she who had mentioned the cab.

'Is she still here?' asked Mr. Budd.

Stayner nodded.

'Send for her,' said the superintendent briefly.

When the frightened woman came, Mr. Budd succeeded in extracting her story from her. Margaret had been out to tea but had returned just before six. Mrs. Billet had been on the point of leaving when the front door bell had rung. She had answered the door and found a man standing on the step. He had inquired for Miss Stayner, saying that he had come from Scotland Yard with a message.

When Margaret had appeared he said that they wanted her at Scotland Yard in connection with the murders at the flat. Superintendent Budd wanted to see her. He apologised for troubling her but he said that it was urgent and he had a cab waiting to take her.

Margaret had left a message for her father and asked Mrs. Billet to stay until she got back. Margaret had left with the man and that was all she could tell.

'What was this man like?' asked Mr. Budd.

The woman was vague.

He was of medium height and dark. She thought he had a moustache but she wasn't sure. The description was so vague as to be practically useless.

'What time did Miss Stayner leave?'

On this point the woman was more definite. It had been a quarter to seven — she had heard Big Ben chime the three quarters — as Margaret left the flat.

'If we'd've sent for her we should have sent a police car,' grunted Mr. Budd, 'but, of course, she wouldn't know that. If this man had a taxi I may be able to get some news of it. I'll come back in a minute.'

He left the greatly worried M.P. pouring out another Johnnie Walker to steady his nerves, and hurried down the stairs and out into Victoria Street. There was one cab on the rank that almost faced the flats. Mr. Budd approached the driver.

'Were you here about a quarter past six?' he asked.

The driver nodded.

'Been 'ere since a quarter to five,' he answered dolefully. 'People don't want cabs much these days. Too expensive for one thing an' there's too much traffic for another. Yer can't get about quickly no more. Where d'yer want to go?'

'I don't want to go anywhere,' said Mr. Budd. He showed the man his warrant card. 'Did you see a taxi stop at that block of flats this evening?'

'Yes, I did. What's up?' said the man.

'Just an inquiry,' answered Mr. Budd. 'Did you notice the number?'

Rather to his surprise the man nodded. He had not only noticed the number but could describe the cab. It was a Renault, rather old-fashioned and painted black. The number was XZ6088.

'You've been a great help,' said Mr. Budd. 'What made you notice this cab?'

The driver chuckled.

'I backs 'orses,' he explained. 'If I sees a car or a cab with four sevens, I knows I'm goin' to be lucky, see?'

As simple as that!

Mr. Budd hurried back to the flats. With a brief explanation to the anxious Stayner, he went to the telephone and rang up the Yard.

'Hello!' he called. 'Superintendent Budd speakin'. I want the Information Room . . . Listen, a girl, Miss Margaret Stayner, has been kidnapped this evening. Warn all stations an' patrol cars to look out for a black Renault taxi, number XZ6088. Pull in the driver and hold him for questioning. Got that? Right! That's all.'

He put down the receiver.

'I'm going back to the Yard,' he said. 'I can't do any good here.'

'Would you like a drink before you go?' asked the M.P. He indicated the Johnnie Walker bottle.

Mr. Budd shook his head.

'You'll let me know directly you've any news?' Stayner asked anxiously as he went with Mr. Budd to the front door.

The big man promised and took his departure. On his way out he called at Gordon Trent's flat but there was no reply to his ring.

When he got back to his office in Scotland Yard, he ordered hot coffee from the canteen and settled down to await any reports that might come in concerning the black Renault, number XZ6088.

At eleven o'clock that night, the driver of a black Renault taxi with that number was picked up by a patrol car and brought to the Yard. Here, he was interviewed by a weary Mr. Budd.

'I picked up this feller near the British Museum,' said the taxi-driver in answer to Mr. Budd's question. 'We went to Wellington Mansions an' I waited until

170

this chap come back with a young lady. They got in the cab an' we drove off . . . '

'Where?' snapped the superintendent.

' 'E told me to go to Waterloo first, then 'e changed his mind an' said to set 'em down in Mecklenburg Square. I thought it was funny, but it weren't no business o' mine.'

'Did the lady make any protest to you?'

The man shook his head.

'No,' he answered.

'She didn't ask you for assistance?'

'No. I thought she looked a bit ill-like,' said the driver.

'Take me to this place where you set them down,' said Mr. Budd, and a few minutes later he was standing in the quiet square.

'It was here, was it?' he asked.

'That's right,' said the taximan. 'There was a car just along there. A blue saloon, it were.'

The stout superintendent walked along the gutter until he came to a small pool of black oil.

'Here?'

The taxi-driver nodded.

The car had evidently waited for some time. There was no proof that Margaret had gone in it, but it seemed probable that she might. The next step was to find out where the car had gone, when it had left Mecklenburg Square.

And that was not going to be easy.

17

Margaret knew that she had been tricked as soon as the taxi had left Wellington Mansions. The man at her side gripped her arm and said in a low voice:

'You'd better do what I tell you. If you try to call out or attract help, I'll kill you. Get that?'

She saw the automatic in his hand and nodded.

'If you behave yourself, you'll be all right,' he said. He let go her arm but he kept the pistol resting on his knee.

He sat in silence until they reached Trafalgar Square and then, leaning forward, he tapped on the window and gave fresh instructions to the driver.

'Why are we going to Mecklenburg Square?' she asked, but he only grunted in reply.

Margaret sat back in the corner of the cab and wondered what she could do. She realised her foolishness in going out with a man she did not know, whatever the excuse. But she hadn't stopped to think. It had seemed quite natural that she should be wanted at Scotland Yard. Would it be any good trying to enlist the help of the driver? A glance sideways showed her the automatic, its muzzle towards her. The man had meant what he said. If she did try to get help, she would be shot.

She opened her handbag and instantly her wrist was gripped.

'What are you up to?' snarled her captor.

'I want my handkerchief . . . '

'I'll get it!' He picked up her bag and thrust his hand inside, feeling about in the interior.

'Here's your handkerchief,' he growled ungraciously. 'I thought you had a gun!'

'Do your female companions usually carry guns?' she asked.

'Never mind what they do!' he snapped. 'You just shut up and do as you're told!'

He relapsed into silence until the taxi stopped. Then he tapped her on the arm.

'Go on, get out,' he ordered, 'and don't

forget what I told you!'

She could have screamed as she got out into the quiet square, but was sensible enough to know that it would do her no good. The taxi-driver was an old man — no match for her captor. If there had been a policeman in sight . . . But, of course, there wasn't!

The man thrust some money into the driver's hand and waited until he had driven away. Then he led her towards a big closed car that waited by the kerb further up on the same side of the square.

He opened the door to the back.

'Get inside!' he ordered. 'Sit in the corner and keep still!'

She did so and he followed her. He said nothing to the silent driver at the wheel but as soon as they were inside, the car moved smoothly forward.

'Where are you taking me?' asked Margaret.

'Don't talk!' retorted the man beside her. 'You'll see, if you wait!'

The car sped onwards and presently they were clear of London. The sweet air of the country came to her nostrils, the heavy scent of flowers from old gardens and the fresh smell of newly turned earth. They were making good speed. The engine ran smoothly and the driver seemed to know exactly where they were going for he never faltered for a second though they followed a twisting course that took them through narrow lanes and little-used tracks.

Presently the car slowed down and she guessed that they must be nearing their destination. The man at her side spoke again:

'I'll give you a word of advice. Don't ask questions. Do as you're told, and keep quiet. That's good advice.'

The car turned through a gateway into a narrow way and the twigs on either side brushed continuously against the sides.

They swung to the left at the end and came upon a low-built house set against a background of straggly trees. Evidently they were expected because as the car came to a stop, the front door of the house opened and a thin man came out. He walked over to the car.

'Everything all right?' he asked.

Margaret's captor nodded curtly.

'Yes, here you are,' he replied. He opened the door and pushed the girl out.

'You come with me,' said the thin man, and to her surprise, instead of going towards the house, he led her down a side path to a high brick wall at the end.

Taking a key from his pocket he opened a heavy door and made her go through into a neglected kitchen garden. At the other end there was a long low-roofed building that looked like stables. He opened another door in this building and Margaret found herself in a brick room with a stone floor.

The place had been roughly furnished. There was a table, a chair, a bed, and a square of matting on the floor. In one corner a tap dripped monotonously.

'Wait here,' said the thin man, pushing her in front of him. 'I may as well warn you that you can scream as much as you like. No one will hear you!'

He turned, went out, and slammed the door behind him. She heard the rasp of a key and the noise of a bolt. There was a dim light burning in the roof. It came from a dusty electric light bulb.

After the thin man had gone, Margaret stood for a moment looking about and then she sat down on the side of the narrow bed.

Up to now she had scarcely thought coherently, but suddenly the full realisation of her situation flooded over her. She was in the hands of the people who had been responsible for the murders in Gordon's flat. What they wanted with her she had not the least idea, but they had tried to get her twice before and there must be some very serious reason to have gone to all this trouble and risk.

She felt physically exhausted and put this down to anxiety and nervous strain. To counteract her tiredness she went over to the dripping tap and bathed her face and hands. The water was icy and she looked round for a towel to dry herself. But there wasn't anything of the kind and she had to make do with a sheet which she pulled from the bed.

She felt a little better, and searched in her handbag for her cigarette-case and matches. Lighting a cigarette, she breathed in the soothing smoke, and tried to think.

She had no idea what they had brought her here for, but she realised that she was in a perilous position. Her first feeling of fear had been replaced by a cold anger. She finished the cigarette and decided to lie down for a few minutes. She must have fallen asleep for the next thing she remembered was sitting up suddenly and hearing the sound of approaching foot-steps.

Almost immediately the bolt was withdrawn and a key rasped in the lock. She stared at the door as it opened and a man came in. He was muffled in a heavy coat and scarf and over his head and face was drawn a woman's nylon stocking.

She crouched back on the narrow bed away from him, and he stood just within the doorway regarding her. The stocking rendered him featureless and hideous.

'So you are Margaret Stayner,' he said in a high-pitched voice, and it was a statement rather than a question.

She stared at him in silence, and closing the door he came nearer.

'I suppose you are wondering why

you've been brought here?' he said after a pause. 'Well, you'll soon know. If you do as you're told you won't be hurt.'

She moistened her lips but she still remained silent.

'Do you understand?' he demanded impatiently.

'What do you want me to say?' she asked.

'I don't want you to say anything,' he answered. 'I want you to write what I shall tell you to write.'

'Supposing I refuse?'

He uttered a queer little laugh.

'I shouldn't advise that,' he said.

'Who are you?' she asked.

He shrugged his shoulders.

'That doesn't matter,' he retorted. 'Do as I ask and you will be allowed to go free. Refuse and you'll never leave here alive!'

He said it in a calm and completely matter-of-fact way that was more menacing than any outburst. It carried conviction.

'What do you want me to write?' she asked, forcing herself to a coolness she was far from feeling.

'I want you to sign a certain document. I have it ready . . . '

'What is it?'

He saw the bewilderment in her face but he did not satisfy her curiosity.

'That doesn't matter,' he said. 'There is no reason why you should know that. All you have to do is to sign it.'

'Are you the man they call Mister Big?'

'I am,' he answered. 'So you know what to expect unless you do as I tell you. I'll fetch the document.'

He turned quickly and went out, locking and bolting the door behind him. She had not expected this abrupt departure. She had imagined that he had brought the document, whatever it was, with him. Apparently, he hadn't.

She expected his return almost at once, but the time went on and he did not come back. After a long time she gave up waiting for him, and dragging the table over to the wall in which there was a barred grille, climbed up and looked out.

It was getting light outside and she could make out a small yard. It was filled with rubbish and weeds and seemed to have been neglected for years.

Almost opposite the barred window

was a tumbledown barn, and by its side a smaller building. Beyond this she could see a high wall crowned with broken splinters of glass.

There was no clue to the locality of her prison, except that it was in the country. Somewhere in the distance she heard a train whistle and the faint rumble of a train. There must be a railway near at hand, but this was little help. England was a network of railways, she could be anywhere.

The light was quite strong and she concluded that she must have slept for longer than she thought. She got down from the table and wandered about the stone room disconsolately. After a while sheer weariness made her sit down.

She tried to imagine what the document could be that the man wanted her to sign. She was still puzzling over this when she fell asleep again. She awoke to see the door shutting. Somebody had come and gone quietly while she slept, leaving behind a tray on the table.

It contained food and tea and the sight of it made her realise how hungry and thirsty she was. She ate the food and drank the tea gratefully.

The sun was up and a thin shaft of its light filtered through the barred window and illuminated a patch of wall.

Nobody came near her. There was no sound of life or movement anywhere, except the occasional rumble of a train. Presently it began to grow dark outside. The dim bulb in the roof had been left burning all the time but its light was faint.

At last there came the sound of whispering voices and the door was opened. The man in the stocking-mask came in followed by the thin man who had received her.

Mister Big took a folded paper from his pocket. Opening it and spreading it out on the table, he pointed to a space at the bottom.

'Here is a pen,' he said, holding it out to her. 'Sign there!'

He kept his hand over part of the document. She hesitated. The thin man was holding an automatic.

'Come on — sign!' repeated Mister Big.

She took the pen from him and went over to the table. And then she saw between his fingers four words.

Last Will and Testament . . .

She flung the pen away with a cry. 'I'll not sign!' she cried. 'I'll not sign!'

18

Gordon Trent had some friends who lived in Bloomsbury. They occupied a tiny flat at the top of one of those new blocks of buildings that are springing up like mushrooms in this district.

Usually Gordon enjoyed an evening with the Lesters and after a restless day during which he had tried to work but found it impossible, he had suddenly made up his mind to go and see them.

Lester and his pretty wife were glad to see him. But Gordon was in one of those peculiar moods when he didn't know what he wanted to do. Five minutes after he arrived at the Lesters, he was searching for an excuse to get away again. He fell back on the age-old excuse of a headache.

He wasn't sure that either of them believed him but it worked. Half an hour after he got there he had left and was walking back to his own flat. He strolled leisurely along, electing to walk through the quiet of Mecklenburg Square. As he came into the square he saw a taxi come round on the other side of the central garden and stop. Without much interest he noted two people get out, a man and a woman, but he was too far away to see them very clearly.

The taxi started again and passed him as it left the square. He noticed the man and the woman walk towards a car that was drawn up near the railings of the central garden. The car was a saloon and as the woman got in he caught a clear view of her face.

It was Margaret Stayner!

Gordon felt his heart quicken. What was the girl doing? Of course she might be with a friend but, after what had happened before, Gordon was a little suspicious. The door of the car was slammed and it began to move away.

Gordon quickened his pace. His instinct told him that something was wrong but he was too far away to do anything. The car gathered speed quickly and swung round out of the square.

Gordon broke into a run. He knew that it was useless to try and keep up with the car but he hoped that he would be lucky enough to find a cab, so that he could follow and find out where Margaret was going.

But there was no cab in sight. The car containing the girl was rapidly vanishing down the road. Gordon stopped and looked up and down. There was no sign of a car of any sort, taxi or otherwise. And then he saw the motor-bicycle!

It was standing outside a house unattended. Gordon didn't hesitate. Here was something that was even better than the cab he had wished for!

A second later he was astride the saddle and kicking frantically at the starter. The engine was warm and sprang to life instantly. Gordon shot off down the road, taking no notice of the shouting behind him.

There was no sign of the car he was pursuing, but he increased his speed, and hoped that it had not got too good a lead. At the end of the road he was in he could see a main thoroughfare. He came out into a broad highway and slowed down, glancing quickly from right to left.

The street he was in he recognised. It was Southampton Row. The question was, which way had the car gone? It was answered almost as soon as it entered his mind.

It was speeding along in the direction of Holborn. He sent the motor-cycle chugging along after it. At Theobald's Road he got into a traffic hold-up and chafed until the lights changed. When he finally got away again the car had disappeared altogether.

He succeeded in picking up the trail again at the junction of Fleet Street and the Strand. The car was heading towards the City and travelling pretty fast. There wasn't a great deal of traffic, and Gordon was able to keep the car easily in sight. He didn't want to overtake it, just find out where it was going.

This excursion of Margaret's might be perfectly legitimate and he didn't want to look a fool. If it wasn't he would be no match for the two men in the car, particularly if they were armed. His best plan was to find out their destination and then notify the police.

He was pretty sure that this was an extension of the two other attempts to get hold of Margaret, and the route the car was taking helped to convince him that he was right.

Reaching the Bank it swung round and headed in the direction of Highbury and Islington and continued on towards Finsbury Park. From there it branched off in the direction of Highgate. Wherever it was going it was taking a circuitous route to get there.

On and on they went along broad highways and narrow byways, through small towns and villages, with Gordon sticking doggedly on behind.

He had by now lost all sense of direction and had no idea whereabouts they were. He prayed that the tank was full of petrol, or at least that there would be enough to last until they reached their destination.

But it wasn't lack of petrol that proved his undoing.

With a loud report his front tyre burst;

the motor-cycle wobbled dangerously, swerved to the side of the road, and landed in a ditch with Gordon underneath it.

The ditch was dry and Gordon was unhurt except for some minor cuts and bruises. Extricating himself from the machine he scrambled to his feet and looked ruefully at the motor-cycle.

The car with Margaret was already out of sight and he wondered what was to be done next. He decided to abandon the useless motor-cycle and continue on foot in the direction the car had been going. He might be able to pick it up again if it was nearing the end of its journey. Anyway, it was the only thing he could do.

He lit a cigarette and set off along the deserted road. It seemed to continue for miles without a break and this was an advantage for the car must have gone straight on.

Presently, however, he came to a turning and hesitated, trying to decide whether to explore this side lane or go straight on. The surface of the road was hard and dry and showed no marks, but going a short distance down the lane he was luckier. There was a slight dip in the surface under some overhanging trees and the ground here was still damp. Plainly visible in this patch were the tyre-marks of a car.

Of course there was nothing to tell him that this was the car containing Margaret, but Gordon decided to risk it. He continued along the lane which grew narrower and narrower as he proceeded. There was no sign of the car but in another damp patch he came upon some more tyre-marks.

Presently the lane swung sharply to the right and ended at a five-barred gate which had been fastened back with a large stone. Beyond this the lane continued, and then again curved sharply to the right.

And there in front of him was the car!

It was drawn up in front of a gap in a straggling hedge and beyond, among some trees, was a house. Gordon proceeded with caution now. There was no sign of anyone near the car and he concluded that Margaret, the driver, and the other man had gone to the house.

He waited concealed by the hedge in case there might be someone still in the car, edging his way nearer until he could see into the interior. It was empty.

Creeping through the gap in the hedge he surveyed the house. It appeared to be uninhabited for the windows were without curtains.

He was undecided what to do next.

Now that he had found out where Margaret had been brought, would it be better to go and invoke the aid of the police? It was the sensible thing to do, but he had no idea where the nearest police station might be. And the search would take time. In the meanwhile, what was happening to Margaret?

He decided to have a look round on his own. He crept stealthily up the neglected path until he could see the house more clearly. In the lower windows were the torn and faded bills of an estate agent advertising the place for sale.

The whole place was neglected and uncared for; the lawn in front was covered with rank grass over a foot high, and what had once been flower-beds were now a tangled wilderness of weeds.

Gordon made a careful circle of the entire building without seeing or hearing any sign of life. Some distance away from the house were a number of outbuildings, as neglected as the rest of the property. From the appearance of these, he concluded that the place had at one time been a small farm. He couldn't see these outbuildings very well because they were enclosed by a high wall. There was a door in this wall but when he tried it, he found that it was locked. Except for the car the whole place might have been empty.

He had to be careful how he explored the place. It was dangerous to go too near in case he should be seen from one of the many windows. Searching round he presently found a spot from whence he could see the front of the house without risk of being seen. It was a small patch of shrubbery, and in the middle of this he took up his position. It was dark now, but there was little he could do except watch. It would have been foolhardy to make any move until he knew what was going on.

In the meantime, he was near at hand and would be able to help Margaret when he had discovered just what was going on.

The hours passed slowly. Gordon grew cramped and stiff, but nothing happened. The house remained still and silent. There was no light to be seen anywhere, and nobody appeared. To add to the unpleasantness of his vigil, he was ravenously hungry.

And then, suddenly, the door opened and a man came out. He was followed by another. The first man, who was tall and thin was saying something to his companion but Gordon was too far away to hear what it was.

They walked round the side of the building, and Gordon followed cautiously. They were making for the door in the wall.

The thin man took a key from his pocket, unlocked the door, and went in, followed by the other man. Gordon hoped that they would leave the door unlocked, and his hope was realised. It opened easily when he tried it.

He slipped cautiously through the door and closed it again behind him. He was in an enclosed patch that had been a kitchen-garden from the look of it. The two men he was following had gone over to one of the outbuildings and he heard a door open and shut.

He waited a moment and then picked his way through the tangled mass of undergrowth towards this building, found the door and listened.

He could hear a faint mumble of voices but nothing of what was being said. Among the deeper tones of the men, however, he heard the lighter voice of a girl. It must be Margaret!

Suddenly the girl's voice rose to a scream and he heard her say:

'I won't sign! I won't sign!'

A heavy blow caught him on the back of the head and he toppled forward, unconscious!

19

He came back to life slowly.

His head was hot and sore and when he tried to raise a hand to his aching forehead he found that it was impossible.

His wrists and ankles had been skilfully tied and he was unable to move. He opened his eyes and looked about. It was a painful process that sent shooting pains through his head.

He was lying on a stone floor in a big brick room that was lighted by a dim bulb in the ceiling. Most of the place was in shadow but he was able to distinguish the four occupants.

They consisted of three men and Margaret!

The girl was sitting on a narrow bed, her face was white and strained and she was staring at a man who had a nylon stocking pulled over his head and face and who was talking in whispers to the other two men. One of these was the tall thin man, the other was short and thick-set. He looked round as Gordon watched and muttered something. The man in the stocking mask came over and looked down.

'Recovered, have you?' he grated. 'You'll be sorry you poked your nose into my business.'

'Not so sorry as you'll be!' retorted Gordon huskily. 'What have you been doing to Miss Stayner?'

'That is no concern of yours,' snapped the man in the stocking mask. 'You've got enough to do to worry about yourself.'

'How long do you think it'll be before the police get here . . . ?'

'Don't try to bluff. It won't get you anywhere.' The man in the mask turned to Margaret. 'Who is this man?'

Margaret remained silent.

'Answer me!' he demanded.

'I'll answer you,' interposed Gordon. 'I'm Gordon Trent. If you don't stop this nonsense . . . '

'So you're Trent, eh? Jameson's friend . . . '

'You're the man they call Mister Big, are you?'

'I'm not wasting any more time,' said

Mister Big. He went over to the shrinking girl. 'Come! Don't let's have any more nonsense. Sign that document!'

'I won't!' she answered. 'It's a will. I won't sign it!'

'You will. And now. I can't wait any longer!'

'You can't make me!' cried Margaret defiantly.

'We'll see about that,' he said softly. 'I think you'll soon change your mind.' He looked over his shoulder. 'Give me a penknife, one of you.'

The thick-set man took a small knife from his pocket and gave it to the other.

'What are you going to do?' he asked curiously.

Mister Big took the knife and pressed open one of the blades.

'You'll see,' he said. 'Got a lighter?'

The thin man produced one.

'Light it,' ordered Mister Big.

The thin man obeyed.

Mister Big held the knife blade in the flame. Gordon watched with a chill in his heart. He guessed what he was going to do and he, Gordon, was powerless to stop it. If only he were free.

He began to strain at the cords at his wrists and ankles. None of them was paying him any attention. They were watching Mister Big . . .

Mister Big turned the blade of the knife in the little flame of the lighter.

'You have beautiful eyes,' he remarked conversationally. 'It would be a pity to destroy them.'

The thin man jerked the lighter away.

'My God, you can't do that!' he protested.

Mister Big turned on him like an angry tiger.

'Hold that lighter up,' he ordered. 'Do as you're told and mind your own business!'

The thin man held up the lighter, but his hands were shaking.

Mister Big turned to the girl.

'Going to change your mind and sign?' he asked.

She could only stare at him in mute horror. In her mind she knew that once she had signed the will nothing could save her life. This man would kill her.

Otherwise there was no object in his insistence that she should sign the will at all.

'The alternative will be very painful,' said Mister Big and advanced the heated blade to within an inch of her left eye.

It was at this moment that Gordon succeeded in getting free. He sprang to his feet and hurled himself on the man in the stocking mask.

The attack was so unexpected that Mister Big staggered and fell. Gordon picked up a lump of brick which he had marked for a weapon and hurled it at the glowing bulb in the ceiling. The bulb exploded with a flash and the room was plunged in darkness.

There was a snarl of rage from the man he had knocked over, and a cry of alarm from the other two. A hand found his throat but Gordon, his temper at boiling-point, lashed out and felt his bunched fist strike flesh. There was a grunt of pain and the fingers at his throat relaxed.

He backed to the wall as someone rushed at him. Again he hit out with all his strength. But this time his fist met only air. He felt his legs gripped and kicked desperately. There was a howl of pain as he recovered his balance.

A circle of white light flashed out. Gordon saw the face of the thin man close to him and drove his right fist at the face, but the man ducked. Gordon struck again, but again the man twisted out of his reach. Then the muzzle of an automatic was thrust into his neck.

'You've caused a lot of trouble,' snarled Mister Big, 'but you won't cause any more!'

Margaret screamed. The report of the pistol and the flash from the muzzle almost split his ear-drum and singed his cheek. But the bullet only chipped a piece out of the wall, for at the moment that Mister Big pressed the trigger there came a thundering banging on the door which spoilt his aim.

'Open this door!' cried a voice authoritatively.

It was the voice of Mr. Budd!

20

Dead silence followed.

Mister Big caught his breath with a sharp hiss. His body stiffened and his hand gripped the butt of the automatic more tightly.

The thin man scrambled to his feet and stared at the door.

'Open this door!'

Mr. Budd's voice sounded peremptory and impatient.

'If you don't open it we shall break it down!'

The words were followed by the thud of a heavy body against the woodwork.

'Put the light out!' breathed Mister Big and the torch was extinguished.

In the darkness Gordon heard the soft movement of his feet and then another sound that puzzled him. A sighing breath that ended in a stifled gasp.

'What was that?' whispered the thin man.

'I caught my foot against something, that's all,' answered Mister Big under his breath. 'Come over here. I want you!'

What the other man answered was drowned in the noise of a rain of blows on the door. The bolts rattled and the wood creaked under the onslaught. But the heavy door held.

Suddenly the noise ceased and there came the mutter of voices from outside. There was a pause and then:

'Now — altogether!'

There was a tremendous crash and a chink of metal on stone as something struck the floor.

That's one of the bolts, thought Gordon. He began to edge his way along the wall towards where he had last seen Margaret. Another crash shook the building and there was the sound of splintering wood.

The next one will do it, thought Gordon. He was right. At the third attack the lock snapped with a report like a pistol shot and the door smashed back on its hinges.

A fan of light split the darkness and the guttural voice of Mister Big cried :

'Keep back — all of you. If you move a step nearer I'll kill the girl!'

He was focused in the white ray of the torch that one of the policemen held, and he was holding the frightened girl in front of him, like a shield, the muzzle of his automatic pressed against her head.

'You'll do better to give in quietly,' said the voice of Mr. Budd calmly. 'You can't get away. You're only makin' matters worse for yourself.'

'Get away from that door,' snapped Mister Big. 'Unless you want to see this girl die!'

'Don't take the risk!' shouted Gordon. 'He means it!'

'Get inside — away from the door. Stand over by the opposite wall!' said the man in the stocking mask. 'Hurry! I've no time to waste!'

'You will have!' retorted Mr. Budd, moving inside the door. The other had the whip-hand and the superintendent knew it. If they didn't do what he demanded Margaret would die. The man was desperate, taking the one chance that offered a possibility of freedom.

Reluctantly he ordered the men who were with him to move over against the wall. As he moved his light shifted and Gordon saw the two men who were lying huddled up on the floor. The grey stone was dappled red.

He remembered that stifled cry in the dark. That had marked the passing of the thick-set man, the other had been killed during the sound of the onslaught on the door. Mr. Budd saw the bodies too.

'They knew too much,' said Mister Big. 'They might have grassed . . . '

'So you killed 'em!' Mr. Budd's voice was hard and stern.

'There was no alternative. Get over there — as far away from the door as possible!'

He moved round as they obeyed, keeping his face with its weird nylon covering towards them. Reaching the open doorway, he backed out.

'Don't try and follow me — if you wish the girl to live!' he said, and disappeared in the darkness, dragging Margaret with him.

'We've got to do something,' began Gordon, but Mr. Budd interrupted him.

'There's nothin' we can do,' he said. 'He's beaten us for the present . . . '

'We can't let Margaret go with him . . . '

'She won't be hurt,' said Mr. Budd. 'He won't take her very far. All he's anxious about at the moment is his own safety. He'll get rid of her as soon as possible. Don't worry!' He went over and looked down at the two dead men on the floor. 'H'm,' he continued, 'I know these fellers. They've been through our hands a good many times. That's 'Snippy' Jackson an' that thin feller's Sam Gates. Cheap little crooks both of 'em.' He looked at Gordon. 'How did you get here?' he asked.

'Look here,' said Gordon. 'Never mind that. What about Margaret . . . ?'

'I tell you she'll be all right,' said the superintendent. 'How did you get here?'

Gordon told him as briefly as possible.

'Where's that document he wanted her to sign?' asked Mr. Budd. 'You say it was a will?'

They made a search but there was no sign of it. Mister Big had taken it with him.

'For God's sake let's stop wasting time!' exclaimed Gordon. 'I'm going after Margaret . . . '

'You'll stay where you are!' ordered Mr. Budd. 'We are doin' all we can do — an' that's nothin'! I know how you're feelin', I'm not feelin' so good myself, but the best thing we can do is wait. I wouldn't be surprised if she wasn't back here pretty soon.'

His prophecy was justified. A stumbling step sounded outside and the dishevelled figure of Margaret almost fell across the threshold.

The next second she was sobbing in Gordon Trent's arms.

★ ★ ★

Gordon volunteered to take the girl back to London. Mr. Budd offered no objection to this, in fact he seemed rather relieved, and one of the men with him was sent to find the nearest police station.

He was instructed to bring back a doctor an ambulance and a police car to take Gordon and Margaret back to London.

While they were waiting for the man's return, Mr. Budd put some questions to the girl about the document she had been asked to sign.

But she was as much puzzled as they. She had no money or property of any kind nor had her father. There seemed no explanation for Mister Big's desperate endeavours to get her signature to a will.

'It's all a bit involved,' agreed Mr. Budd shaking his head dubiously. 'How did this man make his escape? In the car that brought you?'

Margaret nodded.

He had, she explained, taken her with him as far as the car and then let her go. She was obviously suffering from the shock of her experience, and Gordon hoped that it would not be long before he could get her home. She needed rest and lots of it.

It was nearly an hour before the police officer got back, accompanied by a doctor, the local inspector, and a sergeant. The doctor's examination was brief and purely a matter of routine.

'Both these men were stabbed,' he said and Mr. Budd nodded.

'He's fond of the knife,' he remarked. He began to explain to the local men what had happened. Gordon left him to it and took Margaret to the police car that was to transport them back.

When he had gone, Mr. Budd and the local men made a close search of the outbuildings and the house, but nothing of any value to them was found, nor was there anything in the pockets of the dead men to offer a clue.

The house was empty and evidently had been for a number of years. There was dust everywhere and a few articles of broken furniture. Evidently Mister Big had somehow known of the existence of the house and used it for the occasion. Perhaps he had used it before for something.

Mr. Budd was tired and weary by the time they had finished. He accompanied the local inspector to the police station and there concluded the necessary routine jobs that authority demands in the case of murder. The bodies of the two men were taken to the mortuary to await the inquest.

It was with a sigh of relief that the stout superintendent got into the police car which had brought him down and set off for Scotland Yard.

It had been pure accident which had enabled him to arrive on the scene so opportunely. A furious and rather incoherent young man had reported the theft of his motor-bicycle while it had been standing outside a house in Bloomsbury. Mr. Budd might never have heard of this and certainly would never have connected it with Margaret Stayner, but for the fact that when a description of the blue saloon was issued several men on point duty remembered having seen such a car and mentioned the fact that it had been closely followed by a man on a motor-cycle.

A patrolling policeman reported that a saloon car which answered the description of the wanted vehicle had passed him on the St. Albans road travelling at high speed. Again the motor-cycle was mentioned.

Mr. Budd was a little puzzled concerning the motorcyclist, but it helped to identify the car he was after. Patiently in a police car, and accompanied by four of his men, the stout superintendent traced its course.

The last time it had been seen was passing through a small village named Stendon, and after this they lost trace of it entirely. But having got so far, Mr. Budd was determined not to give up.

He cast round, exploring roads and lanes, and came upon the motor-bicycle in the ditch. It hadn't been difficult after that. When they found the car standing outside the gap in the hedge their search was over.

They had tried the house and found it empty, but a number of footprints led to the door in the high wall, and following these had brought them to the outbuilding.

And all the trouble they had taken had been for nothing, thought Mr. Budd wearily, as he lay with closed eyes against the cushions of the police car. It was true they had found the girl, but Mister Big had eluded him. There might never come a chance like that again.

He called in at the Yard to see if there was anything awaiting him that was urgent and ran into Colin Dugan.

'Hello,' greeted the red-haired reporter. 'I've been looking for you . . . '

'I've got nothin' to tell you, an' I'm too tired even to think,' growled Mr. Budd. 'Come back later, much later.'

'Hold on,' persisted Colin. 'I've seen Trent. What do you make of all this will business?'

'I don't!' snapped Mr. Budd. 'It means nothin' to me.'

'What about the car?' asked Colin. 'Have you traced who it belongs to?'

'It belongs to an officer in the Guards,' said Mr. Budd with a tremendous yawn. 'It was stolen from Piccadilly. It was found abandoned in a turnin' off the Strand . . . '

'How do you know that?'

Mr. Budd picked up a slip of paper that lay on his desk.

'Because it says so here,' he replied. 'Now cut along an' leave me alone!'

He sank heavily into the chair behind his desk.

'All right, I'll go,' said Colin. 'Have you tried Somerset House?'

'About this will, d'you mean?' the stout man nodded. 'I'm puttin' a man on to make inquiries. Now get goin'. I want a rest.'

Colin left him slumped in his chair with his hands clasped over his capacious stomach and his eyes closed.

After he had snatched a short sleep, Mr. Budd got up wearily and drove to Wellington Mansions. He found John Stayner in his flat and engaged in packing a suitcase.

'Sit down, superintendent,' said the M.P. 'Will you have a drink?'

He indicated a bottle of Johnnie Walker and glasses on a tray. Mr. Budd shook his head.

'No thank you, sir,' he answered. 'Goin' away?'

'I'm taking my daughter into the country for a few days,' replied Stayner. 'She's had a bad time and it'll do her good. I've got a small cottage near

Godalming. I must thank you for what you did. God knows what would have happened to my little girl if you hadn't turned up in time . . . '

'How is she?' asked Mr. Budd.

'Fast asleep!' answered the M.P. 'Utterly exhausted. Best thing for her. I shan't wake her until it's time for us to leave.'

He shut the suitcase and went over and poured himself out a Johnnie Walker.

'Sure you won't have one?'

'Not at the moment, sir.' Mr. Budd broached the subject which had brought him, but Stayner was unable to help him.

'I can't make it out at all,' he declared. 'I've got a little money — not very much — and that would go to Margaret on my death . . . '

'But she wouldn't get it if she predeceased you,' said Mr. Budd. 'That can't have got anything to do with this will business. You're sure she hasn't inherited any money or property?'

'Quite sure,' asserted Stayner. 'I can't make it out at all . . . '

Mr. Budd pursed his lips.

'Mister Big wouldn't have taken the

214

trouble an' risk unless there was somethin' in it,' he said. 'An' quite a lot in it.'

He left eventually no wiser than when he had come. Getting into the waiting police car, he instructed the driver to go to an address in the city, and settled himself in a corner. The man he was going to see was a lawyer with a none too savoury reputation. He had on more than one occasion come near to being struck off the register. But he knew and had dealings with nearly all the crooks in London. He had helped the police before and there was a chance that he might be able to again. If anyone could find out about this mysterious will Amos Lucas was the man.

He was so completely occupied with his thoughts that he failed to notice the car that was following them. It crept closer until seizing its opportunity it ran alongside the police car.

'Look out!' shouted the driver and Mr. Budd ducked.

He was only just in time. Two muffled reports came from the other car and the window near him splintered as the bullets crashed through the glass and thudded into the upholstery of the seat within a few inches of where Mr. Budd had been sitting!

21

By the time Mr. Budd had recovered from the shock and the driver had stopped the police car, the other car had put on speed and swung into a side turning.

As Mr. Budd scrambled out a police constable came running up, and the usual crowd had gathered round. The stout superintendent briefly explained what had happened, but no one apparently had noticed the number of the car. The only description they got of it was that it was painted dark green and was a Jaguar.

'Probably stolen,' grunted Mr. Budd.

He got back in the police car while the constable moved on the crowd, and continued on his journey. He didn't expect a second attempt but he kept a sharp look out.

A disappointment awaited him when he reached his destination. Mr. Amos Lucas was out of town and would not be back for a week. Gloomily, the stout man returned to the Yard.

Pulling a folder towards him he carefully went over everything that was known about the activities of Mister Big. The actual facts amounted to very little. Although it was common knowledge that Mister Big was the brains behind all the large robberies there was nothing tangible to connect this elusive personality with any of them. It was only from rumours and a number of things let drop by little crooks who had come into the hands of the police, that the existence of the man known as Mister Big was even suspected. But there was definitely someone behind the sharp rise in crime and Mister Big was as good a name as any.

And that was the trouble. He remained only a name.

The first concrete appearance he had made was at Gordon's flat and his efforts to get hold of Margaret Stayner. Also the attempt on the life of John Stayner came into it somewhere. The will! That seemed to be part of a carefully prepared plan. And it must have offered an enormous profit to Mister Big, for he must have been very rich already from the proceeds of the bank raids and other robberies of which he was the instigator.

For the rest of that day and the whole of the one following, Mr. Budd tried to plan a fresh line of action. But he had little to go on. There was still the report of the man who was searching the files at Somerset House, but he had little to go on and the investigation might take time.

On the evening of the third day, just as he was contemplating going home, the telephone rang. It was John Stayner!

'I thought I'd better ring you,' said the M.P., 'but we seem to be having some rather alarming happenings down here.'

'What kind of happenin's?' demanded Mr. Budd sharply.

'There was an attempt to break into the cottage in the early hours of this morning,' answered Stayner. 'It might have been just an ordinary burglar so I didn't say anything. But tonight just after I'd finished tea, I went into the garden, and somebody shot at me from the adjoining wood.'

219

'Shot at you?' repeated Mr. Budd.

'The bullet went unpleasantly close,' said Stayner grimly.

'Where is your cottage?'

'Just off the Godalming road. It's called Willowbend.'

'I'll come down at once,' said Mr. Budd.

He scribbled a note and gave it to a messenger and ordered a car. Ten minutes after he had put down the receiver from John Stayner's call he was on his way to Godalming. Dusk was falling when the car drew to a halt outside the cottage.

It was a low, rambling one-storeyed building, that stood in an acre or so of ground. It was sited half-way down a narrow lane and was enclosed by straggling hedges. There was a miniature wood at the back, but there didn't appear to be a willow tree in sight.

His arrival had been heard for, as he opened the gate to walk up the paved path to the porch, the door opened and the M.P. appeared. His face looked drawn and worried as he greeted Mr. Budd.

'Glad you've come,' he said. 'I don't

like the look of things at all. I tried to phone you again a little while ago to see if you'd left. The wire was cut!'

'Cut!' ejaculated Mr. Budd.

Stayner nodded.

'A whole length taken out of the wire where it runs up the wall of the house,' he said. 'Don't say anything to Margaret.'

He led the way into a comfortable sitting-room. Margaret was sitting in a low chair before the fire reading a book. She looked up as they entered.

'Superintendent Budd has come down to see me about the attempted burglary, dear,' explained Stayner, and she smiled a welcome.

'I'm glad,' she said. 'I was feeling a bit scared. Particularly as the servants have had to be sent to hospital . . . '

Mr. Budd's sleepy eyes narrowed.

'Why was that?' he asked.

'It's a mystery to us,' Stayner said. 'We have two servants here, a man and his wife. They live here permanently. After lunch today they were taken ill. I had to send for a doctor. He thought they were suffering from ptomaine poisoning. They were so ill he had to send them to hospital in an ambulance.'

Mr. Budd felt a slight stirring of his pulses.

Something was brewing!

'So except for myself you're all alone here?' he said.

'And your driver,' said the M.P.

'I didn't bring a driver. I drove myself.'

The stout superintendent was beginning to wish he had brought someone with him. This was a lonely spot. And the telephone was useless!

If Stayner's message hadn't reached him before the phone was put out of action, the M.P. and his daughter would have been alone, at the mercy of whatever was being planned against them.

And something was obviously about to take place that night — something that necessitated the absence of the servants. Mr. Budd felt the bulge of the automatic in his pocket and it was very comforting.

'I expect you'd like a drink after your journey,' said Stayner.

'I think I would,' said Mr. Budd.

'Whisky?'

'Thank you, sir.'

Stayner went over to a side table and poured out two large Johnnie Walkers.

'You'll stay to dinner, won't you?' said Margaret as the M.P. brought the drinks back.

'That's very kind of you — I should like to,' said Mr. Budd.

Stayner was standing by the window, glass in hand. He turned round.

'Bring your drink and let me show you the rest of the cottage,' he said. He gave Mr. Budd a meaning look and the stout man got up. As soon as they were out in the hall, Stayner said :

'I didn't want to alarm my daughter, but there are some men in that wood at the back. I saw them among the trees.'

'How many?' asked Mr. Budd.

Stayner pushed open a door.

'Come in here,' he said. 'You can see for yourself from the dining-room.'

He led the way over to a French window opening on the garden.

'Look!' he said.

They both peered out the window.

'I can't see anythin',' muttered Mr.

Budd. 'It's gettin' pretty dark. Are you sure you weren't mistaken?'

'There were two,' said the M.P. 'I think I saw a third but I wouldn't be certain about that.'

Margaret came in at that moment and put on the light.

'What are you doing in the dark?' she asked in astonishment.

Mr. Budd quickly pulled the curtains across the window.

'We were lookin' at the garden,' he said.

'It's much too dark to see anything,' said the girl. 'I'm going to lay the table. I hope you don't mind a cold meal.'

'Anythin' 'ull do me,' declared Mr. Budd. 'Don't you worry.'

Dinner was not a particularly jovial meal. Stayner was obviously worried although he did his best to hide the fact, and Mr. Budd was alert and watchful. He sensed that there was trouble coming. Margaret kept up the conversation as best she could but she, too, was uneasy and kept looking from one to the other.

It was a relief when the meal was over and they went into the sitting-room for coffee. Stayner produced cigars and a bottle of Hennessy. They sat drinking coffee and brandy and began to feel slightly relaxed.

It had started to rain and the patter of it on the window was the only sound that broke the stillness outside. Margaret was telling Mr. Budd how beautiful it was down here in the summer and how much she preferred it to London, when Stayner held up his hand.

'Listen!' he said sharply.

'What is it?' asked Mr. Budd as the girl broke off.

'I thought I heard something — outside the window,' said the M.P.

Mr. Budd listened but he could hear nothing except the rain which was falling more heavily. And then he *did* hear something. It was the clink of a boot on stone.

'There is someone out there!' cried Stayner and before Mr. Budd could stop him he sprang to his feet and wrenched aside the curtains.

Even as he did so the window flew open with a crash and there appeared framed in the opening three figures, one of which wore a nylon stocking drawn over his head and face.

Margaret uttered a scream and flew to Stayner's side.

'Don't move!' ordered the man in the mask, and Mr. Budd saw that each of the men carried a long-barrelled automatic. 'It'll be the last thing you do, if you do!'

'What is the meaning of this outrage?' said the M.P., his arm round the frightened girl. 'How dare you burst in like this . . . ?'

'Put a sock in it, guv'nor!' snarled one of the men harshly. 'We want the girl.'

Mr. Budd moved his arm and instantly there was a flash and a report. Margaret screamed again as the stout superintendent staggered and fell with a crash that shook the room.

22

Gordon Trent prowled restlessly about his sitting-room. His state of mind was neither conducive to idleness nor work.

He had tried working; had tried reading, but all to no purpose. He couldn't keep his mind from thinking about Margaret and wondering if she was all right. If she had been at home he would have suggested taking her out for the evening. But she wasn't at home. She had gone down to that confounded cottage.

Why had her father wanted to cart her off to that lonely place? Why did people want to go to the country, anyway? It would have done the girl more good to have come out with him, had a good dinner and gone to a show. That's what she wanted, to get over her shock. Not brood all by herself in the depths of the country . . .

And then an idea struck him. Why not get out his small car and run down and see her? Almost before he had thought of the idea he was at the telephone.

But there was no reply to his dialling. After two attempts he called the operator. She tried, but only with the same result.

'I'm sorry, there's no reply.'

'Try again,' snapped Gordon irritably.

There was a lot of buzzing on the line and then another voice broke in:

'This is the supervisor. We cannot get your number. Something is the matter with the line.'

Gordon banged down the receiver. What could have gone wrong with that line? He knew the cottage. He had been down once. It was isolated. And there were only Stayner and the girl there and a couple of old servants.

If there should be another attempt . . . ?

He made up his mind. He would go down to Willowbend and he'd get Colin to go with him. Just in case . . .

He called the *Post-Bulletin* and after a little delay got Colin on the line. The reporter listened to what he had to say.

'It sounds serious to me,' he said gravely. 'We'll go down at once. Pick me up at the office.'

He struggled into his overcoat and went tearing down the stairs and out into Victoria Street. Twenty minutes later he was in Fleet Street.

'There's something up,' said Colin as he squeezed into Gordon's small car. 'I've checked with the exchange. They say Stayner's number is completely unobtainable. It's either a breakdown or . . . '

'Or it's been cut,' finished Gordon.

'Yes, that's about it,' said Colin. 'Come on, get cracking! The quicker we get there the better!' He put his hand in his pocket and took out a revolver. 'It's fully loaded,' he said. 'It'll come in handy if there's any argument!'

'I hope we shan't need it!' said Gordon.

'Be prepared is my motto,' answered Colin. 'Bare fists aren't much use if the other chap's got a gun!'

'We shall probably find them all sitting round drinking coffee,' said Gordon. He spoke lightly but he didn't feel easy. The peculiar instinct which comes to some people now and again and which it is as well to heed because it is nature's warning signal, told him that all was not well. There was danger. He could almost smell it in the air, like you can smell the coming of rain.

He and Colin spoke little during that journey. Each was too occupied with his thoughts to make conversation. The rain started before they left the outskirts of London and by the time they arrived at the cottage it was coming down in sheets. It was Colin who first noticed the police car outside. It was only his warning that stopped Gordon running into it.

'Stupid thing to leave the thing there without lights!' grunted Gordon as he brought his little car to a sudden stop. He got out followed by Colin. 'There are no lights in the house, either.'

'They may be at the back,' said Colin but there was doubt in his tone.

They squelched up the soft path to the front door and Gordon knocked. They waited but there was no reply and he knocked again.

Dead silence! Not a sound from within the dark cottage.

Gordon looked at Colin. What had happened? The occupants couldn't have gone to bed. He knocked again and this time found the bell and rang that as well.

But there was still no reply.

'There can't be anyone in,' muttered Colin. 'You've kicked up enough row to wake the dead.'

He realised that it was an unfortunate simile as soon as he spoke.

'There must be somebody here,' said Gordon. 'They wouldn't go out on a night like this. Besides, there's that car.'

'Let's go round to the back,' said Colin.

They followed a little path that led round through a rustic archway until they came to a small lawn. Gordon stopped suddenly and gripped Colin by the arm.

'Look!' he cried and pointed.

The french window of a room on the ground floor was wide open and one of the glass panes smashed.

'Come on!' said Gordon. He ran to the window. The reporter took a torch from his pocket and played the light about the room beyond. He caught a glimpse of a table laid for a meal and going inside he found an electric switch by the door and switched it on. The light came on and he

231

looked quickly about.

Over near the french window the carpet was stained by the marks of muddy feet, a chair by the table had been overturned, and on the white table-cloth was a great irregular splash of crimson.

'Good God, what has been happening here?' said Gordon huskily. He went to the stain and touched it with his finger. It was blood and it was still wet. With Colin's help he searched the room but there was nothing else.

'Look,' said the red-haired reporter, 'take the car and find the nearest police station. There's one in Godalming. Ask the station sergeant to send someone up here at once. Then ring up the Yard and tell Budd what we found. Be as quick as you can.'

'Can't we save time by trying to find out ourselves what . . . ?'

'No!' broke in Colin firmly. 'Apparently Stayner and his daughter have been carted off somewhere. More than one person must've been involved. Heaven knows where they are but if we find them we shall need help. I'll hold the fort while you're gone, but be quick!'

Without further argument Gordon went out the shattered window. Colin heard his footsteps fade away along the path and later the sound of the car as it started and moved off. He was wondering what he should do to fill in the time until Gordon's return when he saw a spark of light flash for a second in the darkness some distance away.

Instantly he switched out the light. He could see better now. The star-point of light gleamed again, shone for a moment, and then went out.

It came from the midst of a wood at the back of the house that grew almost down to the garden and Colin decided to try and find out who was there with a torch.

The light didn't show again and when he had reached the fringe of trees he paused irresolutely. He listened but he could hear nothing but the drip of the trees. Whoever had been there with the light had gone. But which way had he gone?

Colin stood still, looking from left to right. He almost made up his mind to return to the cottage when he heard a rustle behind him and swung round.

But he was a second too late! A muffled figure loomed out of the wet darkness, a hand gripped him by the throat, and the round muzzle of a pistol was jammed into the back of his neck.

'Got yer!' grunted a menacing voice. 'If you move or make a sound you're as good as dead!'

The voice was the voice of Sergeant Leek!

★   ★   ★

Mr. Budd opened his eyes and stirred uneasily. His head throbbed and at first he could see little. The only light came, so far as he could make out, from a single candle that flickered in a strong draught so that every now and again it almost blew out. He was lying on a bare floor of earth and above his head was the sloping wooden roof of some building.

Several sacks stood in a corner and there was a broken packing case near them. Some of the sacks had burst and grain lay heaped on the floor. In the middle of the floor stood a barrel and on this had been stuck the candle. Standing round this were the men who had broken into the cottage — weird figures in the dim and wavering light, faceless because of the stocking masks that had been pulled over their heads.

Margaret, her eyes wide with fear, was propped up against one wall. She had been securely bound and there was a gag in her mouth. Of John Stayner there was no sign.

What, thought Mr. Budd, had happened to the M.P.?

He was soon to learn.

The door of the barn, for that is what it seemed to be, opened and Mister Big came in. He paused inside the door and turned his head in its nylon covering from side to side.

His eyes through the mask met those of the helpless superintendent.

'Come to your senses, eh?' he said closing the door behind him and moving forward. 'John Stayner was luckier. He didn't!'

He went over to Margaret.

'You're the real reason for all this,' he continued. 'You know what I want from you?'

He took from his pocket a folded paper and signed to one of the other men. He came forward and untied the girl's hands and removed the gag.

'You'd better not scream,' said Mister Big. 'It would not do you any good. This is a very secluded place.'

The girl tried to speak but her mouth was so dry that it was some time before she succeeded.

'Where . . . where is my father?' she whispered huskily.

'Either in heaven or hell,' said Mister Big. 'You can please yourself.'

She shrank back as he put the paper down near her.

'Here is a pen,' he said pushing one into her hand. 'Sign that! And don't let's have any more trouble. I don't want to hurt you . . . ' He stopped but there was no mistaking the threat.

Margaret drew in her breath and bent over the document.

'Where — where do I sign?' she faltered.

'There!' Mister Big pointed, and with difficulty she signed her name.

He snatched up the paper eagerly.

'Re-tie her hands and gag her,' he ordered.

He went over to the barrel and laid the document down beside the flickering candle.

'Two of you come and witness this,' he said. Two of the men came forward and appended their signatures. Mr. Budd wondered what would happen next.

He was soon to learn. Mister Big waited for the ink to dry and then he folded the document and put it carefully away in his pocket.

'Now we can get finished here and go,' he said. He came over to Mr. Budd. 'You won't be troubling me any more, or anyone else. I have always thought that cremation was the most sanitary method of disposing of the dead. It applies to the living as well.'

He swung round to the other men.

'Get the petrol!' he ordered. 'And hurry! The quicker we get away the better.'

From behind the pile of sacks they

brought several cans of petrol.

'Make a good job of it,' said Mister Big. 'Swamp the place thoroughly. It should burn like a bonfire!' He took a torch from his pocket and blew out the candle. 'We don't want a premature conflagration . . . '

'Stop!' A sharp incisive voice cut through the barn. One of the stocking-masked men was covering Mister Big with a long-barrelled automatic.

'What the hell . . . ' began Mister Big furiously, but the other interrupted him.

'I've got a big score to settle with you,' he said. 'It's been piling up for twenty years. I'm going to settle it now!'

At the sound of his voice Mister Big staggered back.

'You know who I am, don't you?' said the man, and tore the stocking mask from his face.

23

The muzzle of the pistol was pressed closer into Colin's neck, and the hand was removed from his throat.

'Now then,' grunted Leek. 'Let's have a look at you. Who are you?'

'I'm Colin Dugan,' gasped the reporter. 'You know me quite well . . . '

Leek opened his mouth wide in astonishment.

'Dugan!' he exclaimed. 'What are yer doin' here?'

'What are you?' demanded Colin. 'Take that thing out of the back of my neck.'

The barrel of the pistol was removed.

'Tell me what you're doin' here?' said the sergeant.

Colin told him.

'Things are beginnin' to move,' said Leek. 'So Mr. Trent's gone to the police, has he? H'm!' he scratched his long chin.

'How long have you been in this wood?' asked the reporter.

'About an hour an' a half,' said Leek. 'I followed a feller down from London. I've been watchin' him for days. He met two other fellers at the station. Well-known crooks they was so I concluded there was somethin' doin'. I was hopin' that they'd give me a line to this Mister Big. But I missed 'em. I traced 'em as far as this wood, an' then they give me the slip. I was havin' a look round when I saw you. I thought I'd got one of 'em.'

He shook his thin head despondently.

'You don't know what happened at the cottage?'

Leek sighed.

'Didn't know there was a cottage,' he said. 'I've been searchin' about in this wood for the past hour . . . '

'Where did you lose sight of the men?' asked Colin.

'Over the other side.' Leek jerked his head in the direction of the far side of the wood. 'About a mile away. I couldn't keep too close to 'em, you see, an' I lost 'em in the wood.'

'Didn't you hear anything while you were looking about?'

'Nothin' at all,' was the lugubrious reply.

'We'd better get back to the cottage,' said Colin. 'We can't do any good here.'

He started to retrace his steps and with a sigh, the melancholy Leek followed. They found the cottage exactly as Colin had left it. They made a thorough search of the place but they found nothing to tell them what had happened to the occupants.

With the exception of the dining-room the rooms were all in order and tidy. They found where the telephone wire had been cut, and Colin was examining this when he heard the sound of a car approaching, and Gordon appeared with an inspector of police and a constable.

'Have you found anything?' he asked eagerly. 'This is Inspector Parsons. I've told him what happened.'

'It looks like a pretty serious business, sir,' said the inspector seriously. 'What do you think happened to these people?'

Colin shook his head.

'I've no idea,' he answered. 'Unless they were taken away by car.'

'In that case there would be traces on the road,' said the inspector. 'Let's see if we can find any.'

They went to the gate but they found nothing — only the marks of Gordon's car.

'That's a police car,' said Leek when he saw the car that Mr. Budd had come in. 'What's it doing here?'

Nobody could answer him. They knew nothing of the superintendent's visit.

They went round to the back of the cottage and examined the ground. On the sodden gravel of the path that bordered the little lawn there was a confused jumble of footprints and the marks of something heavy having been dragged over the grass. The tracks led directly to the wood where Colin had encountered Leek.

'The tracks end here,' said the local inspector. 'It's impossible to follow 'em further among these dead leaves.'

He broke off as he stumbled over something that was hidden by the fallen leaves. It was the body of a man!

Gordon felt the blood drain from his face, and then Leek broke in.

'That's Gould,' he asserted. 'That's the feller I followed from London.'

'He's been tied up,' said the local inspector.

The man was conscious but securely bound. His little pig-like eyes glared up at them and his heavy jaws worked to try and shift the gag that had been wedged in his mouth.

They freed him and took off the gag. The man spat out a lump of turf which it had kept in place and swore fluently.

'That's enough of that!' snapped Inspector Parsons sternly. 'Who tied you up like this?'

'I don't know,' snarled Gould.

'What do you mean, you don't know?'

'What I say. If those swine think they can do a double-cross on me . . . '

'Who are you talking about?' demanded Colin.

A look of cunning spread over the fox-like face.

'Nobody,' he grunted. 'I ain't talking about nobody.'

'That won't wash,' said Leek. 'You came down 'ere for Mister Big, didn't yer? I know because I followed you from London. Come on, you'd better spill it.'

'I'm no grass . . . '

'All right,' said the sergeant. 'Take him along to the cooler. We can charge him with bein' concerned with breakin' into that cottage . . . '

'What are you talking about?' cried Gould. 'I don't know nothin' about a cottage . . . '

'Don't waste time over 'im,' said Leek. 'Get him to the station an' lock him up . . . '

'Look here — I'll tell you what happened if you'll let me go . . . '

'Go on then,' said Leek. 'If your information helps us it'll go in your favour. That's all we can promise you.'

Gould hesitated and then he began to talk. He had been ordered to come to Godalming station and meet another man named Swire from whom he was to receive further instructions. He had done so and been taken to a disused barn where he had been told to put on a stocking mask over his head. He had been told by Swire to go to the edge of the wood that overlooked the cottage and wait there until he was joined by some other men. This he had done, but while he was waiting someone had crept up behind him and knocked him out. That was all he could tell them.

'Sounds a pretty thin story to me,' remarked the melancholy sergeant. 'Where's this nylon stockin' you're supposed to've been wearin'?'

'Whoever knocked me out took that,' snarled Gould.

'Where's this barn?' demanded Gordon.

'On the other side of this wood. Almost in a line from here.'

Colin dragged the man to his feet.

'All right,' he said. 'You can show us.'

The inspector gripped him by the arm.

'Now then,' he said sternly. 'Get a move on!'

They set off through the trees. A quarter of a mile further on they emerged into a clearing. As they did so they heard a sound that brought them to a sudden halt.

Muffled but distinctly audible in the silence of the night came two reports. The sharp staccato bark of an automatic!

Mr. Budd couldn't see the face of the man because he had his back to him, but Mister Big's reaction was swift. He ducked, swept round his arm and knocked over the barrel on which the lighted candle stood, plunging the barn in darkness.

Almost at the same instant a spurt of flame slit the blackness from where he had been a second before. There was a sharp cry. A second stab of flame followed the first, this time from the other man. The two reports came closely together. There was a heavy fall and a smothered groan and then silence. But only for a moment. It was broken by the excited voices and shuffling footsteps as the other men made a panic-stricken rush for the door.

Somebody stumbled over Mr. Budd and cursed loudly. There was a clatter of metal as eager hands groped blindly at the door fastenings, a sudden draught of cold air, and then from outside a shout, and the quick patter of running feet.

A bright beam of light shone out and two more shots drowned out all other sounds. Mr. Budd had a hazy view of struggling figures in the open doorway, silhouetted against the torch light. Then it went out and all was darkness again.

But only for a second. The light flashed out again and played round the inside of the barn. It rested on the bound superintendent, and the man who held it gave an exclamation. He came over and tore the gag from Mr. Budd's mouth.

'Thank you, Dugan,' croaked Mr. Budd. 'Can you cut these infernal ropes?'

Colin pulled a knife from his pocket and slashed through the cords at the superintendent's wrists and ankles. He helped Mr. Budd to his feet, and the stout man rubbed at his legs ruefully.

'Miss Stayner is over there. Go an' see how she is.'

Colin turned but it wasn't needed. Gordon had already found the girl and she was crying on his shoulder.

Mr. Budd looked round. The other men, stripped of the stocking masks, were in the hands of Leek and a constable, brutish-looking ruffians with all the fight gone out of them. Nearby stood another man with a big lump on his forehead.

'Where did he come from?' asked Mr. Budd.

'We brought 'im along with us,' said Leek. 'Found him knocked out in the wood.'

'I see.' Mr. Budd went over to the huddled body by the door. The face was gaunt, the hair close cropped and of the same auburn hue that flamed in the straggling beard. This was the convict — William Sutton. Mr. Budd glanced from him to the man with the bruise on his forehead. He guessed how Sutton had rung the changes . . .

The man was quite dead. The shot from Mister Big as he overturned the barrel had proved fatal.

'Is that the king pippin?' asked Colin at the superintendent's elbow.

Mr. Budd shook his head.

'No,' he answered. 'The king pippin is there.'

He pointed to the man who sprawled across the barrel, his dead fingers still clutching the butt of the automatic in his hand.

'Those two shots in the dark were lucky,' murmured Mr. Budd. He bent down and stripped off the nylon stocking that covered the head and face. Colin gave a startled exclamation.

'It's Stayner!' he cried.

Mr. Budd shook his head.

'That wasn't his real name,' he said. 'His real name was Carlin.' He jerked a thumb in the direction of the body of the bearded man. 'That was the real John Stayner, the girl's father.'

24

It took Mr. Budd nearly two weeks to complete his report — two weeks of hard and patient labour. But at the end of it he had uncovered the mystery of the man known as Mister Big.

'This man, Carlin, to give him his right name, was a crook almost from the time he was born,' Mr. Budd explained in an interview with Colonel Blair. 'He used to smuggle dope and a man named Paget found him out. Carlin killed him, makin' it look as if John Stayner was guilty.

'Paget an' Stayner were partners in a cattle ranch in Canada, and it was here that Carlin first met 'em. When John Stayner's wife died, Stayner came to England with his partner, Paget, for a holiday, and also to find a school for his daughter, Margaret. Nobody knew either of 'em in England. When Stayner was arrested for Paget's murder, he took the name of 'William Sutton' and he was sentenced in that name. He did this to save any stigma attaching to his daughter, although he was quite innocent of the crime.

'It was easy for Carlin to get possession of all Stayner's papers and assume his identity. Paget had left his share of the ranch to his partner, Stayner, so Carlin when he established his identity as Stayner, was fairly well-off. He put a manager in to run the ranch an' drew the profits. The headquarters of Carlin's dope campaign was a warehouse in Upper Thames Street. He owned the freehold but immediately Stayner was sentenced, he sold it to a mythical Henry Goodchild, in reality himself, and then had it transferred again to another fictitious name, the object bein' to stop anyone from tracin' that he was the real owner.

'In his new identity as John Stayner, he had sent the little girl, Margaret, to school and she believed that he was her real father. Stayner had told him once that she would inherit a great deal of property and over two million pounds when she was twenty-one an' he had decided that as soon as she reached that age he would get her to sign a will in his favour and then kill her.

'Meanwhile, he began to build up his criminal connection. As John Stayner he became an M.P. an' under this cloak of respectability he worked up his organisation, until he became known as Mister Big, the unknown planner behind the larger crimes. He was clever, an' he took every precaution to ensure that his identity was unknown to the crooks he employed.

'He had sent Margaret to a school in Germany to get her out of the way, and it was while he was over there to see her, that he met Jameson. Jameson was experimentin' in a method of makin' synthetic cocaine, and Carlin saw what an opportunity such a discovery would make to his drug business. He had almost given it up because of the risk an' difficulty of smugglin' the stuff into the country. But if it could be manufactured it was different.

'He learned that Jameson was coming to England for a holiday, met him an' took him to the warehouse in Upper Thames Street. Here he kept him a prisoner, chained in the cellar, forcing him to perfect his process. He kept him under the influence of the drug as well, but Jameson managed to get free by corrodin' the chain attached to his ankle with a strong acid. He escaped from the warehouse with the fixed intention of findin' his friend, Trent. He reached the flat more dead than alive. Carlin, comin' home from the House, saw him in Victoria Street and recognised him. It must've given him a shock to see him enterin' the very block of flats where he himself lived.'

Mr. Budd paused and cleared his throat.

'The steps he took you know, sir,' he continued. 'He killed Jameson while Trent had gone to fetch the doctor. Then he went up to his own flat and waited until he could slip down the stairs an' pretend that he'd just come in. But the taxi-driver, who knew him, had seen him follow Jameson into the buildin'. He had to silence him, too, and it was a piece of luck for him that the arrival of the girl prevented him talkin' for the moment.

'Carlin had sent her into a carefully prepared trap. She didn't know it but he had got it all fixed. Carlin killed the taxi-driver on his way up to his flat. It was a risk but he had to take it. That's when I first began to wonder about him.'

'You seem to have cleared it up fairly well,' remarked Colonel Blair. 'I don't quite see why he should have gone to all that trouble at the cottage. He could easily have got the girl to sign the will without all that dramatic nonsense.'

'Well, you see, sir,' explained Mr. Budd. 'He knew the story of the will was known. He realised that if the girl died after leavin' him her fortune, he'd be suspected. So he concocted that story about the cottage bein' watched an' the cut wire an' the rest of it. His idea was to make me a witness to the fact that he had nothin' to do with whatever happened to the girl. Mister Big was the man responsible. That's what he wanted us to believe.'

'And what about the men who helped him?' asked the Assistant Commissioner.

'They must have known? They'd have put the black on him for the rest of his life.'

'I don't think any of those men would have lived after they'd finished the job,' said Mr. Budd quietly.

There was a long silence and then the stout superintendent looked across the neat desk at his superior with a faint twinkle in his sleepy eyes.

'Somethin' ought to be done for Sergeant Leek, sir,' he remarked.

Colonel Blair raised his eyebrows slightly.

'Why?' he demanded.

'The loss of his reputation among the crim'nal classes,' said Mr. Budd. 'I made him turn crook. I sent him to night clubs an' such places to drink champagne an' eat caviare an' sell diamond rings at a low price so that it'ud get around to this feller Mister Big's ears, that Leek was crooked an' willin' to accept bribes.'

'Good heavens!' gasped the scandalised Colonel Blair. 'What came of it?'

Mr. Budd chuckled.

'A feller paid Leek twenty pounds to tell him that we were goin' to raid a flat in

Maida Vale on the night we raided the place in Upper Thames Street. I've given it to the Police Orphanage. I think if we hadn't got Mister Big before we should've got him through Leek. The day I was shot at outside here, I had Leek watchin' the entrance in a laundry van. He lost the man who fired the shot, but he did some good work when he followed that feller Gould down to Godalming.'

'Champagne and caviare!' Colonel Blair smoothed a hand across the neat greyness of his hair. 'The expense! And the reputation of the police force . . . '

'It's Sergeant Leek, I'm thinkin' about, sir,' said Mr. Budd sadly. 'He's goin' to miss all that high livin' . . . '

'And a very good thing too,' said the Assistant Commissioner.

★　★　★

Four people sat down to dinner at a secluded table in a little restaurant in Soho. They were a party of laughing people for over six months had elapsed since the tragic night at Willowbend cottage.

Margaret looked radiant. She had overcome all Gordon's objections to marrying a rich woman, and, indeed, had practically proposed to him herself.

'If you don't marry me,' she had threatened. 'I'll give everything away! Now, don't be silly!'

'It'll be like marrying the Bank of England,' said Gordon, 'but if that's what you wish . . . ?'

'I do!' declared Margaret.

'We're getting married on the ninth,' said Gordon. 'Margaret thinks that long engagements are a mistake.'

Colin Dugan, looking unusually clean and tidy, grinned.

'Much better get the thing over and done with,' he said. 'Once it's done you can't get out of it.'

'That's just the kind of thing you *would* say!' declared Eileen Barnard indignantly.

'Don't you agree with me?' Colin looked surprised. 'Anyway, I think the ninth's an excellent date. Why not make it a foursome?'

'What do you mean?' asked Gordon. 'Who are the other two?'

'Me and Eileen!' said Colin calmly and ungrammatically.

Eileen stared at him.

'Why you haven't even asked me,' she began.

'Haven't I?' said Colin. 'Oh, well, here goes. What about it, eh?'

'Well, I don't know,' she began.

'Listen, woman!' said Colin. 'You'll marry me on the ninth — and like it!'

THE END

THE FACELESS ONES
GRIM DEATH
MURDER IN MANUSCRIPT
THE GLASS ARROW
THE THIRD KEY
THE ROYAL FLUSH MURDERS
THE SQUEALER
MR. WHIPPLE EXPLAINS
THE SEVEN CLUES
THE CHAINED MAN
THE HOUSE OF THE GOAT
THE FOOTBALL POOL MURDERS
THE HAND OF FEAR
SORCERER'S HOUSE
THE HANGMAN
THE CON MAN

We do hope that you have enjoyed reading this large print book.

Did you know that all of our titles are available for purchase?

We publish a wide range of high quality large print books including:
Romances, Mysteries, Classics
General Fiction
Non Fiction and Westerns

Special interest titles available in large print are:
The Little Oxford Dictionary
Music Book, Song Book
Hymn Book, Service Book

Also available from us courtesy of Oxford University Press:
Young Readers' Dictionary
(large print edition)
Young Readers' Thesaurus
(large print edition)

For further information or a free brochure, please contact us at:
Ulverscroft Large Print Books Ltd.,
The Green, Bradgate Road, Anstey,
Leicester, LE7 7FU, England.
Tel: (00 44) 0116 236 4325
Fax: (00 44) 0116 234 0205

Other titles in the
Linford Mystery Library:

THE DOCTOR'S DAUGHTER

Sally Quilford

Whilst the Great War rages in Europe, sleepy Midchester is pitched into a mystery when a man is found dead in an abandoned house. Twenty-four-year-old Peg Bradbourne is well on the way to becoming a spinster detective, but it is a role she is reluctant to accept. When her stepmother also dies in suspicious circumstances, Peg makes a promise to her younger sister, putting aside her own misgivings in order to find out the truth.

SERGEANT CRUSOE

Leslie Wilkie

Luke Sharp is unaware that he has a double — Marco Da Silva, the ruthless criminal gang leader known as 'Silver'. When a pair of vigilantes intent on taking their revenge against Silver shoot Luke by mistake, his life is changed dramatically. Convalescing at his grandfather's home, he agrees to transcribe the old man's wartime memoirs of his exploits in the South Pacific. However, Silver finds out about Luke, and attempts to coerce him into work as his double in crime . . .

HOUSE OF FOOLS

V. J. Banis

Toby Stewart has been invited by her sister Anne to visit her at Fool's End, the manor where she works as a personal secretary to a famous author, and after his recent death has stayed on to catalogue his papers and manuscripts. But on arriving, Toby is dismayed to learn that Anne has mysteriously disappeared — without taking any of her possessions and without informing her employers. And most everyone there, it seems, has something to hide. Did Anne leave of her own volition — or has she perhaps been murdered . . . ?

DEATH VISITS KEMPSHOTT HOUSE

Katherine Hutton

Nick Shaw, travel writer and enthusiastic archer, expects to spend an enjoyable weekend with his partner, Louisa, at the luxurious Kempshott House Hotel. Then a body is discovered during an archery club contest on the hotel's grounds, stuck through with three arrows. The police are called in, assisted by Louisa — a detective sergeant — and it soon becomes apparent that the man has been deliberately murdered. Worse still, it would appear that the murderer hasn't finished yet . . .

TWELVE HOURS TO DESTINY

Manning K. Robertson

At the height of the Cold War one of the most trusted and important British agents in Hong Kong, Chao Lin, suddenly vanishes, and in London Steve Carradine is put on the case. Now hints are filtering through to Hong Kong of a new weapon with which the Chinese hope to dominate the world, and Chao Lin is the only man outside of China to possess this vital information. Carradine's assignment is simple: Find Chao Lin, discover the nature of this secret weapon, and bring both out of China!